# TO BUILD A FIRE

AND

TALES OF THE NORTH

"I laugh at you and your strength. Strike, and strike hard."

JACK LONDON STATE HISTORIC PARK

*Jack London*

# TO BUILD A FIRE

AND

## TALES OF THE NORTH

BY

JACK LONDON

ILLUSTRATED WORKS OF JACK LONDON
PUBLISHED BY

SEAWOLF
PRESS

**TO BUILD A FIRE AND TALES OF THE NORTH**


**PUBLISHED BY SEAWOLF PRESS**

Printed in the U.S.A.

**EDITION INFORMATION**
These stories were variously published in serial format in magazines and later in the books *Lost Face, The Son of the Wolf, The Faith of Men, Children of the Frost,* and *Love of Life.*

**SeaWolf Press**
P.O. Box 961
Orinda, CA 94563
Email: support@seawolfpress.com
Web: http://www.SeaWolfPress.com

**About *To Build a Fire and Tales of the North***

A wonderful collection of seven stories by Jack London. The all-time classic story, "To Build a Fire", tells of survival in the unforgiving wilderness. A solo newcomer ignores the advice of old-timers and travels alone in sub-zero temperatures where survival may depend on your ability to start a fire. This collection also includes "Lost Face" which tells of a trapper ingenuously trying to avoid torture at the hands of his captors. "The One Thousand Dozen" examines the importance of eggs in the far north.

**About Jack London**

Jack London lived a life of extremes while becoming the best known author in the world. Raised in a working class family in Oakland, California, he was primarily self-taught. His adventurous life provided material for his stories, articles, and books. Known for his realistic writing, his life experiences are revealed in every book. He spent time as a teenage oyster pirate on San Francisco Bay, sailed on a sealing schooner, train-hopped the country as a hobo, scrambled for gold in the Klondike, sailed the Pacific, and was heavily involved in socialism. His dream house in Glen Ellen burned to the ground the day it was finished.

# Books by Jack London

COLLECT ALL THESE SPECIAL SEAWOLF PRESS EDITIONS

Son of the Wolf (1900)
The God of His Fathers (1901)
Children of the Frost (1902)
The Cruise of the Dazzler (1902)
A Daughter of the Snows (1902)
Kempton-Wace Letters (1903)
The Call of the Wild (1903)
The People of the Abyss (1903)
The Faith of Men (1904)
The Sea-Wolf (1904)
War of the Classes (1905)
The Game (1905)
Tales of the Fish Patrol (1905)
Moon-Face (1906)
White Fang (1906)
Scorn of Women (1906)
Before Adam (1907)
Love of Life (1907)
The Road (1907)
The Iron Heel (1908)
Martin Eden (1909)
Lost Face (1910)
Revolution (1910)
Burning Daylight (1910)
Theft (1910)
When God Laughs (1911)
Adventure (1911)
The Cruise of the Snark (1911)
South Sea Tales (1911)
The House of Pride (1912)
A Son of the Sun (1912)
Smoke Bellew (1912)
The Night Born (1913)
The Abysmal Brute (1913)
John Barleycorn (1913)
The Valley of the Moon (1913)
The Strength of the Strong (1914)
The Mutiny of the Elsinore (1914)
The Scarlet Plague (1915)
The Star Rover (1915)
Little Lady of the Big House (1916)
The Acorn Planter (1916)
The Turtles of Tasman (1916)
The Human Drift (1917)
Jerry of the Islands (1917)
Michael, Brother of Jerry (1917)
The Red One (1918)
On the Makaloa Mat (1919)
Hearts of Three (1920)
Dutch Courage (1922)

# CONTENTS

# LOST FACE

It was the end. Subienkow had travelled a long trail of bitterness and horror, homing like a dove for the capitals of Europe, and here, farther away than ever, in Russian America, the trail ceased. He sat in the snow, arms tied behind him, waiting the torture. He stared curiously before him at a huge Cossack, prone in the snow, moaning in his pain. The men had finished handling the giant and turned him over to the women. That they exceeded the fiendishness of the men, the man's cries attested.

Subienkow looked on, and shuddered. He was not afraid to die. He had carried his life too long in his hands, on that weary trail from Warsaw to Nulato, to shudder at mere dying. But he objected to the torture. It offended his soul. And this offence, in turn, was not due to the mere pain he must endure, but to the sorry spectacle the pain would make of him. He knew that he would pray, and beg, and entreat, even as Big Ivan and the others that had gone before. This would not be nice. To pass out bravely and cleanly, with a smile and a jest—ah! that would have been the way. But to lose control, to have his soul upset by the pangs of the flesh, to screech and gibber like an ape, to become the veriest beast—ah, that was what was so terrible.

There had been no chance to escape. From the beginning, when he dreamed the fiery dream of Poland's independence, he had become a puppet in the hands of Fate. From the beginning, at Warsaw, at St. Petersburg, in the Siberian mines, in Kamtchatka, on the crazy boats of the fur-thieves, Fate had been driving him to this end. Without doubt, in the foundations of the world was graved this end for him—for him, who was so fine and sensitive, whose nerves scarcely sheltered under his skin, who was a dreamer, and a poet, and an artist. Before he was dreamed of, it had been determined that the quivering bundle of sensitiveness that constituted him should be doomed to live in raw and howling savagery, and to die in this far land of night, in this dark place beyond the last boundaries of the world.

He sighed. So that thing before him was Big Ivan—Big Ivan the giant, the man without nerves, the man of iron, the Cossack turned freebooter of the seas, who was as phlegmatic as an ox, with a nervous system so low that what was pain to ordinary men was scarcely a tickle to him. Well, well, trust these Nulato Indians to find Big Ivan's nerves and trace them to the roots of his quivering soul. They were certainly doing it. It was inconceivable that a man could suffer so much and yet live. Big Ivan was paying for his low order of nerves. Already he had lasted twice as long as any of the others.

Subienkow felt that he could not stand the Cossack's sufferings much longer. Why didn't Ivan die? He would go mad if that screaming did not cease. But when it did cease, his turn would come. And there was Yakaga awaiting him, too, grinning at him even now in anticipation—Yakaga, whom only last week he had kicked out of the fort, and upon whose face he had laid the lash of his dog-whip. Yakaga would attend to him. Doubtlessly Yakaga was saving for him more refined tortures, more exquisite nerve-racking. Ah! that must have been a good one, from the way Ivan screamed. The squaws bending over him stepped back with laughter and clapping of hands. Subienkow saw the monstrous thing that had been perpetrated, and began to laugh hysterically. The Indians looked at him in wonderment that he should laugh. But Subienkow could not stop.

This would never do. He controlled himself, the spasmodic twitchings slowly dying away. He strove to think of other things, and began reading back in his own life. He remembered his mother and his father, and the little spotted pony, and the French tutor who had taught him dancing and sneaked him an old worn copy of Voltaire. Once more he saw Paris, and dreary London, and gay Vienna, and Rome. And once more he saw that wild group of youths who had dreamed, even as he, the dream of an independent Poland with a king of Poland on the throne at Warsaw. Ah, there it was that the long trail began. Well, he had lasted longest. One by one, beginning with the two executed at St. Petersburg, he took up the count of the passing of those brave spirits. Here one had been beaten to death by a jailer, and there, on that bloodstained highway of the exiles, where they had marched for endless months, beaten and maltreated by their Cossack guards, another had dropped by the way. Always it had been savagery—brutal, bestial savagery. They had died—of fever, in the mines, under the knout. The last two had died after the escape, in the battle with the Cossacks, and he alone had won to Kamtchatka with the stolen papers and the money of a traveller he had left lying in the snow.

It had been nothing but savagery. All the years, with his heart in studios, and theatres, and courts, he had been hemmed in by savagery. He had purchased his life with blood. Everybody had killed. He had killed that traveller for his passports. He had proved that he was a man of parts by duelling with two Russian officers on a single day. He had had to prove himself in order to win to a place among the fur-thieves. He had had to win to that place. Behind him lay the thousand-years-long road across all Siberia and Russia. He could not escape that way. The only way was ahead, across the dark and icy sea of Bering to Alaska. The way had led from savagery to deeper savagery. On the scurvy-rotten ships of the fur-thieves, out of food and out of water, buffeted by the interminable storms of that stormy sea, men had become animals. Thrice he had sailed east from Kamtchatka. And thrice, after all manner of hardship and suffering, the survivors had come back to Kamtchatka. There had been no outlet for escape, and he could not go back the way he had come, for the mines and the knout awaited him.

Again, the fourth and last time, he had sailed east. He had been with those who first found the fabled Seal Islands; but he had not returned with them to share the wealth of furs in the mad orgies of Kamtchatka. He had sworn never to go back. He knew that to win to those dear capitals of Europe he must go on. So he had changed ships and remained in the dark new land. His comrades were Slavonian hunters and Russian adventurers, Mongols and Tartars and Siberian aborigines; and through the savages of the new world they had cut a path of blood. They had massacred whole villages that refused to furnish the fur-tribute; and they, in turn, had been massacred by ships' companies. He, with one Finn, had been the sole survivor of such a company. They had spent a winter of solitude and starvation on a lonely Aleutian isle, and their rescue in the spring by another fur-ship had been one chance in a thousand.

But always the terrible savagery had hemmed him in. Passing from ship to ship, and ever refusing to return, he had come to the ship that explored south. All down the Alaska coast they had encountered nothing but hosts of savages. Every anchorage among the beetling islands or under the frowning cliffs of the mainland had meant a battle or a storm. Either the gales blew, threatening destruction, or the war canoes came off, manned by howling natives with the war-paint on their faces, who came to learn the bloody virtues of the sea-rovers' gunpowder. South, south they had coasted, clear to the myth-land of California. Here, it was said, were Spanish adventurers who had fought their way up from Mexico. He had had hopes of those Spanish adventurers. Escaping to them, the rest would have been easy—a year or two, what did it matter more or less—and he would win to Mexico, then a ship, and Europe would be his. But they had met no Spaniards. Only had they encountered the same impregnable wall of savagery. The denizens of the confines of the world, painted for war, had driven them back from the shores. At last, when one boat was cut off and every man killed, the commander had abandoned the quest and sailed back to the north.

The years had passed. He had served under Tebenkoff when Michaelovski Redoubt was built. He had spent two years in the Kuskokwim country. Two summers, in the month of June, he had managed to be at the head of Kotzebue Sound. Here, at this time, the tribes assembled for barter; here were to be found spotted deerskins from Siberia, ivory from the Diomedes, walrus skins from the shores of the Arctic, strange stone lamps, passing in trade from tribe to tribe, no one knew whence, and, once, a hunting-knife of English make; and here, Subienkow knew, was the school in which to learn geography. For he met Eskimos from Norton Sound, from King Island and St. Lawrence Island, from Cape Prince of Wales, and Point Barrow. Such places had other names, and their distances were measured in days.

It was a vast region these trading savages came from, and a vaster region from which, by repeated trade, their stone lamps and that steel knife had come. Subienkow bullied, and cajoled, and bribed. Every far-journeyer or strange tribesman was brought before him. Perils unaccountable and unthinkable were mentioned, as well as wild beasts, hostile tribes, impenetrable forests, and mighty mountain ranges; but always from beyond came the rumour and the tale of white-skinned men, blue of eye and fair of hair, who fought like devils and who sought always for furs. They were to the east—far, far to the east. No one had seen them. It was the word that had been passed along.

It was a hard school. One could not learn geography very well through the medium of strange dialects, from dark minds that mingled fact and fable and that measured distances by "sleeps" that varied according to the difficulty of the going. But at last came the whisper that gave Subienkow courage. In the east lay a great river where were these blue-eyed men. The river was called the Yukon. South of Michaelovski Redoubt emptied another great river which the Russians knew as the Kwikpak. These two rivers were one, ran the whisper.

Subienkow returned to Michaelovski. For a year he urged an expedition up the Kwikpak. Then arose Malakoff, the Russian half-breed, to lead the wildest and most ferocious of the hell's broth of mongrel adventurers who had crossed from Kamtchatka. Subienkow was his lieutenant. They threaded the mazes of the great delta of the

Kwikpak, picked up the first low hills on the northern bank, and for half a thousand miles, in skin canoes loaded to the gunwales with trade-goods and ammunition, fought their way against the five-knot current of a river that ran from two to ten miles wide in a channel many fathoms deep. Malakoff decided to build the fort at Nulato. Subienkow urged to go farther. But he quickly reconciled himself to Nulato. The long winter was coming on. It would be better to wait. Early the following summer, when the ice was gone, he would disappear up the Kwikpak and work his way to the Hudson Bay Company's posts. Malakoff had never heard the whisper that the Kwikpak was the Yukon, and Subienkow did not tell him.

Came the building of the fort. It was enforced labour. The tiered walls of logs arose to the sighs and groans of the Nulato Indians. The lash was laid upon their backs, and it was the iron hand of the freebooters of the sea that laid on the lash. There were Indians that ran away, and when they were caught they were brought back and spread-eagled before the fort, where they and their tribe learned the efficacy of the knout. Two died under it; others were injured for life; and the rest took the lesson to heart and ran away no more. The snow was flying ere the fort was finished, and then it was the time for furs. A heavy tribute was laid upon the tribe. Blows and lashings continued, and that the tribute should be paid, the women and children were held as hostages and treated with the barbarity that only the fur-thieves knew.

Well, it had been a sowing of blood, and now was come the harvest. The fort was gone. In the light of its burning, half the fur-thieves had been cut down. The other half had passed under the torture. Only Subienkow remained, or Subienkow and Big Ivan, if that whimpering, moaning thing in the snow could be called Big Ivan. Subienkow caught Yakaga grinning at him. There was no gainsaying Yakaga. The mark of the lash was still on his face. After all, Subienkow could not blame him, but he disliked the thought of what Yakaga would do to him. He thought of appealing to Makamuk, the head-chief; but his judgment told him that such appeal was useless. Then, too, he thought of bursting his bonds and dying fighting. Such an end would be quick. But he could not break his bonds. Caribou thongs were stronger than he. Still devising, another thought came to him. He signed for Makamuk, and that an interpreter who knew the coast dialect should be brought.

"Oh, Makamuk," he said, "I am not minded to die. I am a great man, and it were foolishness for me to die. In truth, I shall not die. I am not like these other carrion."

He looked at the moaning thing that had once been Big Ivan, and stirred it contemptuously with his toe.

"I am too wise to die. Behold, I have a great medicine. I alone know this medicine. Since I am not going to die, I shall exchange this medicine with you."

"What is this medicine?" Makamuk demanded.

"It is a strange medicine."

Subienkow debated with himself for a moment, as if loth to part with the secret.

"I will tell you. A little bit of this medicine rubbed on the skin makes the skin hard like a rock, hard like iron, so that no cutting weapon can cut it. The strongest blow of a cutting weapon is a vain thing against it. A bone knife becomes like a piece of mud; and it will turn the edge of the iron knives we have brought among you. What will you give me for the secret of the medicine?"

"I will give you your life," Makamuk made answer through the interpreter.

Subienkow laughed scornfully.

"And you shall be a slave in my house until you die."

The Pole laughed more scornfully.

"Untie my hands and feet and let us talk," he said.

The chief made the sign; and when he was loosed Subienkow rolled a cigarette and lighted it.

"This is foolish talk," said Makamuk. "There is no such medicine. It cannot be. A cutting edge is stronger than any medicine."

The chief was incredulous, and yet he wavered. He had seen too many deviltries of fur-thieves that worked. He could not wholly doubt.

"I will give you your life; but you shall not be a slave," he announced.

"More than that."

Subienkow played his game as coolly as if he were bartering for a foxskin.

"It is a very great medicine. It has saved my life many times. I want a sled and dogs, and six of your hunters to travel with me down the river and give me safety to one day's sleep from Michaelovski Redoubt."

"You must live here, and teach us all of your deviltries," was the reply.

Subienkow shrugged his shoulders and remained silent. He blew cigarette smoke out on the icy air, and curiously regarded what remained of the big Cossack.

"That scar!" Makamuk said suddenly, pointing to the Pole's neck, where a livid mark advertised the slash of a knife in a Kamtchatkan brawl. "The medicine is not good. The cutting edge was stronger than the medicine."

"It was a strong man that drove the stroke." (Subienkow considered.) "Stronger than you, stronger than your strongest hunter, stronger than he."

Again, with the toe of his moccasin, he touched the Cossack—a grisly spectacle, no longer conscious—yet in whose dismembered body the pain-racked life clung and was loth to go.

"Also, the medicine was weak. For at that place there were no berries of a certain kind, of which I see you have plenty in this country. The medicine here will be strong."

"I will let you go down river," said Makamuk; "and the sled and the dogs and the six hunters to give you safety shall be yours."

"You are slow," was the cool rejoinder. "You have committed an offence against my medicine in that you did not at once accept my terms. Behold, I now demand more. I want one hundred beaver skins." (Makamuk sneered.)

"I want one hundred pounds of dried fish." (Makamuk nodded, for fish were plentiful and cheap.) "I want two sleds—one for me and one for my furs and fish. And my rifle must be returned to me. If you do not like the price, in a little while the price will grow."

Yakaga whispered to the chief.

"But how can I know your medicine is true medicine?" Makamuk asked.

"It is very easy. First, I shall go into the woods—"

Again Yakaga whispered to Makamuk, who made a suspicious dissent.

"You can send twenty hunters with me," Subienkow went on. "You see, I must get the berries and the roots with which to make the medicine. Then, when you have brought the two sleds and loaded on them the fish and the beaver skins and the rifle, and when you have told off the six hunters who will go with me—then, when all is ready, I will rub the medicine on my neck, so, and lay my neck there on that log. Then can your strongest hunter take the axe and strike three times on my neck. You yourself can strike the three times."

Makamuk stood with gaping mouth, drinking in this latest and most wonderful magic of the fur-thieves.

"But first," the Pole added hastily, "between each blow I must put on fresh medicine. The axe is heavy and sharp, and I want no mistakes."

"All that you have asked shall be yours," Makamuk cried in a rush of acceptance. "Proceed to make your medicine."

Subienkow concealed his elation. He was playing a desperate game, and there must be no slips. He spoke arrogantly.

"You have been slow. My medicine is offended. To make the offence clean you must give me your daughter."

He pointed to the girl, an unwholesome creature, with a cast in one eye and a bristling wolf-tooth. Makamuk was angry, but the Pole remained imperturbable, rolling and lighting another cigarette.

"Make haste," he threatened. "If you are not quick, I shall demand yet more."

In the silence that followed, the dreary northland scene faded before him, and he saw once more his native land, and France, and, once, as he glanced at the wolf-toothed girl, he remembered another girl, a singer and a dancer, whom he had known when first as a youth he came to Paris.

"What do you want with the girl?" Makamuk asked.

"To go down the river with me." Subienkow glanced over her critically. "She will make a good wife, and it is an honour worthy of my medicine to be married to your blood."

Again he remembered the singer and dancer and hummed aloud a song she had taught him. He lived the old life over, but in a detached, impersonal sort of way, looking at the memory-pictures of his own life as if they were pictures in a book of anybody's life. The chief's voice, abruptly breaking the silence, startled him

"It shall be done," said Makamuk. "The girl shall go down the river with you. But be it understood that I myself strike the three blows with the axe on your neck."

"But each time I shall put on the medicine," Subienkow answered, with a show of ill-concealed anxiety.

"You shall put the medicine on between each blow. Here are the hunters who shall see you do not escape. Go into the forest and gather your medicine."

Makamuk had been convinced of the worth of the medicine by the Pole's rapacity. Surely nothing less than the greatest of medicines could enable a man in the shadow of death to stand up and drive an old-woman's bargain.

"Besides," whispered Yakaga, when the Pole, with his guard, had disappeared among the spruce trees, "when you have learned the medicine you can easily destroy him."

"But how can I destroy him?" Makamuk argued. "His medicine will not let me destroy him."

"There will be some part where he has not rubbed the medicine," was Yakaga's reply. "We will destroy him through that part. It may be his ears. Very well; we will thrust a spear in one ear and out the other. Or it may be his eyes. Surely the medicine will be much too strong to rub on his eyes."

The chief nodded. "You are wise, Yakaga. If he possesses no other devil-things, we will then destroy him."

Subienkow did not waste time in gathering the ingredients for his medicine, he selected whatsoever came to hand such as spruce needles, the inner bark of the willow, a strip of birch bark, and a quantity of moss-berries, which he made the hunters dig up for him from beneath the snow. A few frozen roots completed his supply, and he led the way back to camp.

Makamuk and Yakaga crouched beside him, noting the quantities and kinds of the ingredients he dropped into the pot of boiling water.

"You must be careful that the moss-berries go in first," he explained.

"And—oh, yes, one other thing—the finger of a man. Here, Yakaga, let me cut off your finger."

But Yakaga put his hands behind him and scowled.

"Just a small finger," Subienkow pleaded.

"Yakaga, give him your finger," Makamuk commanded.

"There be plenty of fingers lying around," Yakaga grunted, indicating the human wreckage in the snow of the score of persons who had been tortured to death.

"It must be the finger of a live man," the Pole objected.

"Then shall you have the finger of a live man." Yakaga strode over to the Cossack and sliced off a finger.

"He is not yet dead," he announced, flinging the bloody trophy in the snow at the Pole's feet. "Also, it is a good finger, because it is large."

Subienkow dropped it into the fire under the pot and began to sing. It was a French love-song that with great solemnity he sang into the brew.

"Without these words I utter into it, the medicine is worthless," he explained. "The words are the chiefest strength of it. Behold, it is ready."

"Name the words slowly, that I may know them," Makamuk commanded.

"Not until after the test. When the axe flies back three times from my neck, then will I give you the secret of the words."

"But if the medicine is not good medicine?" Makamuk queried anxiously.

Subienkow turned upon him wrathfully.

"My medicine is always good. However, if it is not good, then do by me as you have done to the others. Cut me up a bit at a time, even as you have cut him up." He pointed to the Cossack. "The medicine is now cool. Thus, I rub it on my neck, saying this further medicine."

With great gravity he slowly intoned a line of the "Marseillaise," at the same time rubbing the villainous brew thoroughly into his neck.

An outcry interrupted his play-acting. The giant Cossack, with a last resurgence of his tremendous vitality, had arisen to his knees. Laughter and cries of surprise and applause arose from the Nulatos, as Big Ivan began flinging himself about in the snow with mighty spasms.

Subienkow was made sick by the sight, but he mastered his qualms and made believe to be angry.

"This will not do," he said. "Finish him, and then we will make the test. Here, you, Yakaga, see that his noise ceases."

While this was being done, Subienkow turned to Makamuk.

"And remember, you are to strike hard. This is not baby-work. Here, take the axe and strike the log, so that I can see you strike like a man."

Makamuk obeyed, striking twice, precisely and with vigour, cutting out a large chip.

"It is well." Subienkow looked about him at the circle of savage faces that somehow seemed to symbolize the wall of savagery that had hemmed him about ever since the Czar's police had first arrested him in Warsaw. "Take your axe, Makamuk, and stand so. I shall lie down. When I raise my hand, strike, and strike with all your might. And be careful that no one stands behind you. The medicine is good, and the axe may bounce from off my neck and right out of your hands."

He looked at the two sleds, with the dogs in harness, loaded with furs and fish. His rifle lay on top of the beaver skins. The six hunters who were to act as his guard stood by the sleds.

"Where is the girl?" the Pole demanded. "Bring her up to the sleds before the test goes on."

When this had been carried out, Subienkow lay down in the snow, resting his head on the log like a tired child about to sleep. He had lived so many dreary years that he was indeed tired.

"I laugh at you and your strength, O Makamuk," he said. "Strike, and strike hard."

He lifted his hand. Makamuk swung the axe, a broadaxe for the squaring of logs. The bright steel flashed through the frosty air, poised for a perceptible instant above Makamuk's head, then descended upon Subienkow's bare neck. Clear through flesh and bone it cut its way, biting deeply into the log beneath. The amazed savages saw the head bounce a yard away from the blood-spouting trunk.

There was a great bewilderment and silence, while slowly it began to dawn in their minds that there had been no medicine. The fur-thief had outwitted them. Alone, of all their prisoners, he had escaped the torture. That had been the stake for which he played. A great roar of laughter went up. Makamuk bowed his head in shame. The fur-thief had fooled him. He had lost face before all his people. Still they continued to roar out their laughter. Makamuk turned, and with bowed head stalked away. He knew that thenceforth he would be no longer known as Makamuk. He would be Lost Face; the record of his shame would be with him until he died; and whenever the tribes gathered in the spring for the salmon, or in the summer for the trading, the story would pass back and forth across the camp-fires of how the fur-thief died peaceably, at a single stroke, by the hand of Lost Face.

"Who was Lost Face?" he could hear, in anticipation, some insolent young buck demand, "Oh, Lost Face," would be the answer, "he who once was Makamuk in the days before he cut off the fur-thief's head."

## TO BUILD A FIRE

Day had broken cold and grey, exceedingly cold and grey, when the man turned aside from the main Yukon trail and climbed the high earth-bank, where a dim and little-travelled trail led eastward through the fat spruce timberland. It was a steep bank, and he paused for breath at the top, excusing the act to himself by looking at his watch. It was nine o'clock. There was no sun nor hint of sun, though there was not a cloud in the sky. It was a clear day, and yet there seemed an intangible pall over the face of things, a subtle gloom that made the day dark, and that was due to the absence of sun. This fact did not worry the man. He was used to the lack of sun. It had been days since he had seen the sun, and he knew that a few more days must pass before that cheerful orb, due south, would just peep above the sky-line and dip immediately from view.

The man flung a look back along the way he had come. The Yukon lay a mile wide and hidden under three feet of ice. On top of this ice were as many feet of snow. It was all pure white, rolling in gentle undulations where the ice-jams of the freeze-up had formed. North and south, as far as his eye could see, it was unbroken white, save for a dark hair-line that curved and twisted from around the spruce-covered island to the south, and that curved and twisted away into the north, where it disappeared behind another spruce-covered island. This dark hair-line was the trail—the main trail—that led south five hundred miles to the Chilcoot Pass, Dyea, and salt water; and that led north seventy miles to Dawson, and still on to the north a thousand miles to Nulato, and finally to St. Michael on Bering Sea, a thousand miles and half a thousand more.

But all this—the mysterious, far-reaching hairline trail, the absence of sun from the sky, the tremendous cold, and the strangeness and weirdness of it all—made no impression on the man. It was not because he was long used to it. He was a new-comer in the land, a *chechaquo*, and this was his first winter. The trouble with him was that he was without imagination. He was quick and alert in the things of life, but only in the things, and not in the significances. Fifty degrees below zero meant eighty odd degrees of frost. Such fact impressed him as being cold and uncomfortable, and that was all. It did not lead him to meditate upon his frailty as a creature of temperature, and upon man's frailty in general, able only to live within certain narrow limits of heat and cold; and from there on it did not lead him to the conjectural field of immortality and man's place in the universe. Fifty degrees below zero stood for a bite of frost that hurt and that must be guarded against by the use of mittens, earflaps, warm moccasins, and thick socks. Fifty degrees below zero was to him just precisely fifty degrees below zero. That there should be anything more to it than that was a thought that never entered his head.

As he turned to go on, he spat speculatively. There was a sharp, explosive crackle that startled him. He spat again. And again, in the air, before it could fall to the snow, the spittle crackled. He knew that at fifty below spittle crackled on the snow, but this spittle had crackled in the air. Undoubtedly it was colder than fifty below—

how much colder he did not know. But the temperature did not matter. He was bound for the old claim on the left fork of Henderson Creek, where the boys were already. They had come over across the divide from the Indian Creek country, while he had come the roundabout way to take a look at the possibilities of getting out logs in the spring from the islands in the Yukon. He would be in to camp by six o'clock; a bit after dark, it was true, but the boys would be there, a fire would be going, and a hot supper would be ready. As for lunch, he pressed his hand against the protruding bundle under his jacket. It was also under his shirt, wrapped up in a handkerchief and lying against the naked skin. It was the only way to keep the biscuits from freezing. He smiled agreeably to himself as he thought of those biscuits, each cut open and sopped in bacon grease, and each enclosing a generous slice of fried bacon.

He plunged in among the big spruce trees. The trail was faint. A foot of snow had fallen since the last sled had passed over, and he was glad he was without a sled, travelling light. In fact, he carried nothing but the lunch wrapped in the handkerchief. He was surprised, however, at the cold. It certainly was cold, he concluded, as he rubbed his numbed nose and cheek-bones with his mittened hand. He was a warm-whiskered man, but the hair on his face did not protect the high cheek-bones and the eager nose that thrust itself aggressively into the frosty air.

At the man's heels trotted a dog, a big native husky, the proper wolf-dog, grey-coated and without any visible or temperamental difference from its brother, the wild wolf. The animal was depressed by the tremendous cold. It knew that it was no time for travelling. Its instinct told it a truer tale than was told to the man by the man's judgment. In reality, it was not merely colder than fifty below zero; it was colder than sixty below, than seventy below. It was seventy-five below zero. Since the freezing-point is thirty-two above zero, it meant that one hundred and seven degrees of frost obtained. The dog did not know anything about thermometers. Possibly in its brain there was no sharp consciousness of a condition of very cold such as was in the man's brain. But the brute had its instinct. It experienced a vague but menacing apprehension that subdued it and made it slink along at the man's heels, and that made it question eagerly every unwonted movement of the man as if expecting him to go into camp or to seek shelter somewhere and build a fire. The dog had learned fire, and it wanted fire, or else to burrow under the snow and cuddle its warmth away from the air.

The frozen moisture of its breathing had settled on its fur in a fine powder of frost, and especially were its jowls, muzzle, and eyelashes whitened by its crystalled breath. The man's red beard and moustache were likewise frosted, but more solidly, the deposit taking the form of ice and increasing with every warm, moist breath he exhaled. Also, the man was chewing tobacco, and the muzzle of ice held his lips so rigidly that he was unable to clear his chin when he expelled the juice. The result was that a crystal beard of the color and solidity of amber was increasing its length on his chin. If he fell down it would shatter itself, like glass, into brittle fragments. But he did not mind the appendage. It was the penalty all tobacco-chewers paid in that country, and he had been out before in two cold snaps. They had not been so cold as this, he knew, but by the spirit thermometer at Sixty Mile he knew they had been registered at fifty below and at fifty-five.

He held on through the level stretch of woods for several miles, crossed a wide flat of nigger-heads, and dropped down a bank to the frozen bed of a small stream. This was Henderson Creek, and he knew he was ten miles from the forks. He looked at his watch. It was ten o'clock. He was making four miles an hour, and he calculated that he would arrive at the forks at half-past twelve. He decided to celebrate that event by eating his lunch there.

The dog dropped in again at his heels, with a tail drooping discouragement, as the man swung along the creek-bed. The furrow of the old sled-trail was plainly visible, but a dozen inches of snow covered the marks of the last runners. In a month no man had come up or down that silent creek. The man held steadily on. He was not much given to thinking, and just then particularly he had nothing to think about save that he would eat lunch at the forks and that at six o'clock he would be in camp with the boys. There was nobody to talk to and, had there been, speech would have been impossible because of the ice-muzzle on his mouth. So he continued monotonously to chew tobacco and to increase the length of his amber beard.

Once in a while the thought reiterated itself that it was very cold and that he had never experienced such cold. As he walked along he rubbed his cheek-bones and nose with the back of his mittened hand. He did this automatically, now and again changing hands. But rub as he would, the instant he stopped his cheek-bones went numb, and the following instant the end of his nose went numb. He was sure to frost his cheeks; he knew that, and experienced a pang of regret that he had not devised a nose-strap of the sort Bud wore in cold snaps. Such a strap passed across the cheeks, as well, and saved them. But it didn't matter much, after all. What were frosted cheeks? A bit painful, that was all; they were never serious.

Empty as the man's mind was of thoughts, he was keenly observant, and he noticed the changes in the creek, the curves and bends and timber-jams, and always he sharply noted where he placed his feet. Once, coming around a bend, he shied abruptly, like a startled horse, curved away from the place where he had been walking, and retreated several paces back along the trail. The creek he knew was frozen clear to the bottom—no creek could contain water in that arctic winter—but he knew also that there were springs that bubbled out from the hillsides and ran along under the snow and on top the ice of the creek. He knew that the coldest snaps never froze these springs, and he knew likewise their danger. They were traps. They hid pools of water under the snow that might be three inches deep, or three feet. Sometimes a skin of ice half an inch thick covered them, and in turn was covered by the snow. Sometimes there were alternate layers of water and ice-skin, so that when one broke through he kept on breaking through for a while, sometimes wetting himself to the waist.

That was why he had shied in such panic. He had felt the give under his feet and heard the crackle of a snow-hidden ice-skin. And to get his feet wet in such a temperature meant trouble and danger. At the very least it meant delay, for he would be forced to stop and build a fire, and under its protection to bare his feet while he dried his socks and moccasins. He stood and studied the creek-bed and its banks, and decided that the flow of water came from the right. He reflected awhile, rubbing his nose and cheeks, then skirted to the left, stepping gingerly and testing the footing for each step. Once clear of the danger, he took a fresh chew of tobacco and swung along at his four-mile gait.

In the course of the next two hours he came upon several similar traps. Usually the snow above the hidden pools had a sunken, candied appearance that advertised the danger. Once again, however, he had a close call; and once, suspecting danger, he compelled the dog to go on in front. The dog did not want to go. It hung back until the man shoved it forward, and then it went quickly across the white, unbroken surface. Suddenly it broke through, floundered to one side, and got away to firmer footing. It had wet its forefeet and legs, and almost immediately the water that clung to it turned to ice. It made quick efforts to lick the ice off its legs, then dropped down in the snow and began to bite out the ice that had formed between the toes. This was a matter of instinct. To permit the ice to remain would mean sore feet. It did not know this. It merely obeyed the mysterious prompting that arose from the deep crypts of its being. But the man knew, having achieved a judgment on the subject, and he removed the mitten from his right hand and helped tear out the ice-particles. He did not expose his fingers more than a minute, and was astonished at the swift numbness that smote them. It certainly was cold. He pulled on the mitten hastily, and beat the hand savagely across his chest.

At twelve o'clock the day was at its brightest. Yet the sun was too far south on its winter journey to clear the horizon. The bulge of the earth intervened between it and Henderson Creek, where the man walked under a clear sky at noon and cast no shadow. At half-past twelve, to the minute, he arrived at the forks of the creek. He was pleased at the speed he had made. If he kept it up, he would certainly be with the boys by six. He unbuttoned his jacket and shirt and drew forth his lunch. The action consumed no more than a quarter of a minute, yet in that brief moment the numbness laid hold of the exposed fingers. He did not put the mitten on, but, instead, struck the fingers a dozen sharp smashes against his leg. Then he sat down on a snow-covered log to eat. The sting that followed upon the striking of his fingers against his leg ceased so quickly that he was startled, he had had no chance to take a bite of biscuit. He struck the fingers repeatedly and returned them to the mitten, baring the other hand for the purpose of eating. He tried to take a mouthful, but the ice-muzzle prevented. He had forgotten to build a fire and thaw out. He chuckled at his foolishness, and as he chuckled he noted the numbness creeping into the exposed fingers. Also, he noted that the stinging which had first come to his toes when he sat down was already passing away. He wondered whether the toes were warm or numbed. He moved them inside the moccasins and decided that they were numbed.

He pulled the mitten on hurriedly and stood up. He was a bit frightened. He stamped up and down until the stinging returned into the feet. It certainly was cold, was his thought. That man from Sulphur Creek had spoken the truth when telling how cold it sometimes got in the country. And he had laughed at him at the time! That showed one must not be too sure of things. There was no mistake about it, it was cold. He strode up and down, stamping his feet and threshing his arms, until reassured by the returning warmth. Then he got out matches and proceeded to make a fire. From the undergrowth, where high water of the previous spring had lodged a supply of seasoned twigs, he got his firewood. Working carefully from a small beginning, he soon had a roaring fire, over which he thawed the ice from his face and in the protection of which he ate his biscuits. For the moment the cold of space was outwitted. The dog took satisfaction in the fire, stretching out close enough for warmth and far enough away to escape being singed.

When the man had finished, he filled his pipe and took his comfortable time over a smoke. Then he pulled on his mittens, settled the ear-flaps of his cap firmly about his ears, and took the creek trail up the left fork. The dog was disappointed and yearned back toward the fire. This man did not know cold. Possibly all the generations of his ancestry had been ignorant of cold, of real cold, of cold one hundred and seven degrees below freezing-point. But the dog knew; all its ancestry knew, and it had inherited the knowledge. And it knew that it was not good to walk abroad in such fearful cold. It was the time to lie snug in a hole in the snow and wait for a curtain of cloud to be drawn across the face of outer space whence this cold came. On the other hand, there was keen intimacy between the dog and the man. The one was the toil-slave of the other, and the only caresses it had ever received were the caresses of the whip-lash and of harsh and menacing throat-sounds that threatened the whip-lash. So the dog made no effort to communicate its apprehension to the man. It was not concerned in the welfare of the man; it was for its own sake that it yearned back toward the fire. But the man whistled, and spoke to it with the sound of whip-lashes, and the dog swung in at the man's heels and followed after.

The man took a chew of tobacco and proceeded to start a new amber beard. Also, his moist breath quickly powdered with white his moustache, eyebrows, and lashes. There did not seem to be so many springs on the left fork of the Henderson, and for half an hour the man saw no signs of any. And then it happened. At a place where there were no signs, where the soft, unbroken snow seemed to advertise solidity beneath, the man broke through. It was not deep. He wetted himself half-way to the knees before he floundered out to the firm crust.

He was angry, and cursed his luck aloud. He had hoped to get into camp with the boys at six o'clock, and this would delay him an hour, for he would have to build a fire and dry out his foot-gear. This was imperative at that low temperature—he knew that much; and he turned aside to the bank, which he climbed. On top, tangled in the underbrush about the trunks of several small spruce trees, was a high-water deposit of dry firewood—sticks and twigs principally, but also larger portions of seasoned branches and fine, dry, last-year's grasses. He threw down several large pieces on top of the snow. This served for a foundation and prevented the young flame from drowning itself in the snow it otherwise would melt. The flame he got by touching a match to a small shred of birch-bark that he took from his pocket. This burned even more readily than paper. Placing it on the foundation, he fed the young flame with wisps of dry grass and with the tiniest dry twigs.

He worked slowly and carefully, keenly aware of his danger. Gradually, as the flame grew stronger, he increased the size of the twigs with which he fed it. He squatted in the snow, pulling the twigs out from their entanglement in the brush and feeding directly to the flame. He knew there must be no failure. When it is seventy-five below zero, a man must not fail in his first attempt to build a fire—that is, if his feet are wet. If his feet are dry, and he fails, he can run along the trail for half a mile and restore his circulation. But the circulation of wet and freezing feet cannot be restored by running when it is seventy-five below. No matter how fast he runs, the wet feet will freeze the harder.

All this the man knew. The old-timer on Sulphur Creek had told him about it the previous fall, and now he was appreciating the advice. Already all sensation had gone out of his feet. To build the fire he had been forced to remove his mittens, and the fingers had quickly gone numb. His pace of four miles an hour had kept his heart pumping blood to the surface of his body and to all the extremities. But the instant he stopped, the action of the pump eased down. The cold of space smote the unprotected tip of the planet, and he, being on that unprotected tip, received the full force of the blow. The blood of his body recoiled before it. The blood was alive, like the dog, and like the dog it wanted to hide away and cover itself up from the fearful cold. So long as he walked four miles an hour, he pumped that blood, willy-nilly, to the surface; but now it ebbed away and sank down into the recesses of his body. The extremities were the first to feel its absence. His wet feet froze the faster, and his exposed fingers numbed the faster, though they had not yet begun to freeze. Nose and cheeks were already freezing, while the skin of all his body chilled as it lost its blood.

But he was safe. Toes and nose and cheeks would be only touched by the frost, for the fire was beginning to burn with strength. He was feeding it with twigs the size of his finger. In another minute he would be able to feed it with branches the size of his wrist, and then he could remove his wet foot-gear, and, while it dried, he could keep his naked feet warm by the fire, rubbing them at first, of course, with snow. The fire was a success. He was safe. He remembered the advice of the old-timer on Sulphur Creek, and smiled. The old-timer had been very serious in laying down the law that no man must travel alone in the Klondike after fifty below. Well, here he was; he had had the accident; he was alone; and he had saved himself. Those old-timers were rather womanish, some of them, he thought. All a man had to do was to keep his head, and he was all right. Any man who was a man could travel alone. But it was surprising, the rapidity with which his cheeks and nose were freezing. And he had not thought his fingers could go lifeless in so short a time. Lifeless they were, for he could scarcely make them move together to grip a twig, and they seemed remote from his body and from him. When he touched a twig, he had to look and see whether or not he had hold of it. The wires were pretty well down between him and his finger-ends.

All of which counted for little. There was the fire, snapping and crackling and promising life with every dancing flame. He started to untie his moccasins. They were coated with ice; the thick German socks were like sheaths of iron half-way to the knees; and the mocassin strings were like rods of steel all twisted and knotted as by some conflagration. For a moment he tugged with his numbed fingers, then, realizing the folly of it, he drew his sheath-knife.

But before he could cut the strings, it happened. It was his own fault or, rather, his mistake. He should not have built the fire under the spruce tree. He should have built it in the open. But it had been easier to pull the twigs from the brush and drop them directly on the fire. Now the tree under which he had done this carried a weight of snow on its boughs. No wind had blown for weeks, and each bough was fully freighted. Each time he had pulled a twig he had communicated a slight agitation to the tree—an imperceptible agitation, so far as he was concerned, but an agitation sufficient to bring about the disaster. High up in the tree one bough capsized its load of snow. This fell on the boughs beneath, capsizing them. This process continued, spreading out and involving the whole tree. It grew like an avalanche, and it descended without warning upon the man and the fire, and the fire was blotted out! Where it had burned was a mantle of fresh and disordered snow.

The man was shocked. It was as though he had just heard his own sentence of death. For a moment he sat and stared at the spot where the fire had been. Then he grew very calm. Perhaps the old-timer on Sulphur Creek was right. If he had only had a trail-mate he would have been in no danger now. The trail-mate could have built the fire. Well, it was up to him to build the fire over again, and this second time there must be no failure. Even if he succeeded, he would most likely lose some toes. His feet must be badly frozen by now, and there would be some time before the second fire was ready.

Such were his thoughts, but he did not sit and think them. He was busy all the time they were passing through his mind, he made a new foundation for a fire, this time in the open; where no treacherous tree could blot it out. Next, he gathered dry grasses and tiny twigs from the high-water flotsam. He could not bring his fingers together to pull them out, but he was able to gather them by the handful. In this way he got many rotten twigs and bits of green moss that were undesirable, but it was the best he could do. He worked methodically, even collecting an armful of the larger branches to be used later when the fire gathered strength. And all the while the dog sat and watched him, a certain yearning wistfulness in its eyes, for it looked upon him as the fire-provider, and the fire was slow in coming.

When all was ready, the man reached in his pocket for a second piece of birch-bark. He knew the bark was there, and, though he could not feel it with his fingers, he could hear its crisp rustling as he fumbled for it. Try as he would, he could not clutch hold of it. And all the time, in his consciousness, was the knowledge that each instant his feet were freezing. This thought tended to put him in a panic, but he fought against it and kept calm. He pulled on his mittens with his teeth, and threshed his arms back and forth, beating his hands with all his might against his sides. He did this sitting down, and he stood up to do it; and all the while the dog sat in the snow, its wolf-brush of a tail curled around warmly over its forefeet, its sharp wolf-ears pricked forward intently as it watched the man. And the man as he beat and threshed with his arms and hands, felt a great surge of envy as he regarded the creature that was warm and secure in its natural covering.

After a time he was aware of the first far-away signals of sensation in his beaten fingers. The faint tingling grew stronger till it evolved into a stinging ache that was excruciating, but which the man hailed with satisfaction. He stripped the mitten from his right hand and fetched forth the birch-bark. The exposed fingers were quickly going numb again. Next he brought out his bunch of sulphur matches. But the tremendous cold had already driven the life out of his fingers. In his effort to separate one match from the others, the whole bunch fell in the snow. He tried to pick it out of the snow, but failed. The dead fingers could neither touch nor clutch. He was very careful. He drove the thought of his freezing feet; and nose, and cheeks, out of his mind, devoting his whole soul to the matches. He watched, using the sense of vision in place of that of touch, and when he saw his fingers on each side the bunch, he closed them—that is, he willed to close them, for the wires were drawn, and the fingers did not obey. He pulled the mitten on the right hand, and beat it fiercely against his knee. Then, with both mittened hands, he scooped the bunch of matches, along with much snow, into his lap. Yet he was no better off.

After some manipulation he managed to get the bunch between the heels of his mittened hands. In this fashion he carried it to his mouth. The ice crackled and snapped when by a violent effort he opened his mouth. He drew the lower jaw in, curled the upper lip out of the way, and scraped the bunch with his upper teeth in order to separate a match. He succeeded in getting one, which he dropped on his lap. He was no better off. He could not pick it up. Then he devised a way. He picked it up in his teeth and scratched it on his leg. Twenty times he scratched before he succeeded in lighting it. As it flamed he held it with his teeth to the birch-bark. But the burning brimstone went up his nostrils and into his lungs, causing him to cough spasmodically. The match fell into the snow and went out.

The old-timer on Sulphur Creek was right, he thought in the moment of controlled despair that ensued: after fifty below, a man should travel with a partner. He beat his hands, but failed in exciting any sensation. Suddenly he bared both hands, removing the mittens with his teeth. He caught the whole bunch between the heels of his hands. His arm-muscles not being frozen enabled him to press the hand-heels tightly against the matches. Then he scratched the bunch along his leg. It flared into flame, seventy sulphur matches at once! There was no wind to blow them out. He kept his head to one side to escape the strangling fumes, and held the blazing bunch to the birch-bark. As he so held it, he became aware of sensation in his hand. His flesh was burning. He could smell it. Deep down below the surface he could feel it. The sensation developed into pain that grew acute. And still he endured it, holding the flame of the matches clumsily to the bark that would not light readily because his own burning hands were in the way, absorbing most of the flame.

At last, when he could endure no more, he jerked his hands apart. The blazing matches fell sizzling into the snow, but the birch-bark was alight. He began laying dry grasses and the tiniest twigs on the flame. He could not pick and choose, for he had to lift the fuel between the heels of his hands. Small pieces of rotten wood and green moss clung to the twigs, and he bit them off as well as he could with his teeth. He cherished the flame carefully and awkwardly. It meant life, and it must not perish. The withdrawal of blood from the surface of his body now made him begin to shiver, and he grew more awkward. A large piece of green moss fell squarely on the little fire. He tried to poke it out with his fingers, but his shivering frame made him poke too far, and he disrupted the nucleus of the little fire, the burning grasses and tiny twigs separating and scattering. He tried to poke them together again, but in spite of the tenseness of the effort, his shivering got away with him, and the twigs were hopelessly scattered. Each twig gushed a puff of smoke and went out. The fire-provider had failed. As he looked apathetically about him, his eyes chanced on the dog, sitting across the ruins of the fire from him, in the snow, making restless, hunching movements, slightly lifting one forefoot and then the other, shifting its weight back and forth on them with wistful eagerness.

The sight of the dog put a wild idea into his head. He remembered the tale of the man, caught in a blizzard, who killed a steer and crawled inside the carcass, and so was saved. He would kill the dog and bury his hands in the warm body until the numbness went out of them. Then he could build another fire. He spoke to the dog, calling it to him; but in his voice was a strange note of fear that frightened the animal, who had never known the man to speak in such way before. Something was the matter, and its suspicious nature sensed danger,—it knew not what danger but somewhere, somehow, in its brain arose an apprehension of the man. It flattened its ears down at the sound of the man's voice, and its restless, hunching movements and the liftings and shiftings of its forefeet became more pronounced but it would not come to the man. He got on his hands and knees and crawled toward the dog. This unusual posture again excited suspicion, and the animal sidled mincingly away.

The man sat up in the snow for a moment and struggled for calmness. Then he pulled on his mittens, by means of his teeth, and got upon his feet. He glanced down at first in order to assure himself that he was really standing up, for the absence of sensation in his feet left him unrelated to the earth. His erect position in itself started to drive the webs of suspicion from the dog's mind; and when he spoke peremptorily, with the sound of whip-lashes in his voice, the dog rendered its customary allegiance and came to him. As it came within reaching distance, the man lost his control. His arms flashed out to the dog, and he experienced genuine surprise when he discovered that his hands could not clutch, that there was neither bend nor feeling in the lingers. He had forgotten for the moment that they were frozen and that they were freezing more and more. All this happened quickly, and before the animal could get away, he encircled its body with his arms. He sat down in the snow, and in this fashion held the dog, while it snarled and whined and struggled.

But it was all he could do, hold its body encircled in his arms and sit there. He realized that he could not kill the dog. There was no way to do it. With his helpless hands he could neither draw nor hold his sheath-knife nor throttle the animal. He released it, and it plunged wildly away, with tail between its legs, and still snarling. It halted forty feet away and surveyed him curiously, with ears sharply pricked forward. The man looked down at his hands in order to locate them, and found them hanging on the ends of his arms. It struck him as curious that one should have to use his eyes in order to find out where his hands were. He began threshing his arms back and forth, beating the mittened hands against his sides. He did this for five minutes, violently, and his heart pumped enough blood up to the surface to put a stop to his shivering. But no sensation was aroused in the hands. He had an impression that they hung like weights on the ends of his arms, but when he tried to run the impression down, he could not find it.

A certain fear of death, dull and oppressive, came to him. This fear quickly became poignant as he realized that it was no longer a mere matter of freezing his fingers and toes, or of losing his hands and feet, but that it was a matter of life and death with the chances against him. This threw him into a panic, and he turned and ran up the creek-bed along the old, dim trail. The dog joined in behind and kept up with him. He ran blindly, without intention, in fear such as he had never known in his life. Slowly, as he ploughed and floundered through the snow, he began to see things again—the banks of the creek, the old timber-jams, the leafless aspens, and the sky. The running made him feel better. He did not shiver. Maybe, if he ran on, his feet would thaw out; and, anyway, if he ran far enough, he would reach camp and the boys. Without doubt he would lose some fingers and toes and some of his face; but the boys would take care of him, and save the rest of him when he got there. And at the same time there was another thought in his mind that said he would never get to the camp and the boys; that it was too many miles away, that the freezing had too great a start on him, and that he would soon be stiff and dead. This thought he kept in the background and refused to consider. Sometimes it pushed itself forward and demanded to be heard, but he thrust it back and strove to think of other things.

It struck him as curious that he could run at all on feet so frozen that he could not feel them when they struck the earth and took the weight of his body. He seemed to himself to skim along above the surface and to have no connection with the earth. Somewhere he had once seen a winged Mercury, and he wondered if Mercury felt as he felt when skimming over the earth.

His theory of running until he reached camp and the boys had one flaw in it: he lacked the endurance. Several times he stumbled, and finally he tottered, crumpled up, and fell. When he tried to rise, he failed. He must sit and rest, he decided, and next time he would merely walk and keep on going. As he sat and regained his breath, he noted that he was feeling quite warm and comfortable.

He was not shivering, and it even seemed that a warm glow had come to his chest and trunk. And yet, when he touched his nose or cheeks, there was no sensation. Running would not thaw them out. Nor would it thaw out his hands and feet. Then the thought came to him that the frozen portions of his body must be extending. He tried to keep this thought down, to forget it, to think of something else; he was aware of the panicky feeling that it caused, and he was afraid of the panic. But the thought asserted itself, and persisted, until it produced a vision of his body totally frozen. This was too much, and he made another wild run along the trail. Once he slowed down to a walk, but the thought of the freezing extending itself made him run again.

And all the time the dog ran with him, at his heels. When he fell down a second time, it curled its tail over its forefeet and sat in front of him facing him curiously eager and intent. The warmth and security of the animal angered him, and he cursed it till it flattened down its ears appeasingly. This time the shivering came more quickly upon the man. He was losing in his battle with the frost. It was creeping into his body from all sides. The thought of it drove him on, but he ran no more than a hundred feet, when he staggered and pitched headlong. It was his last panic. When he had recovered his breath and control, he sat up and entertained in his mind the conception of meeting death with dignity. However, the conception did not come to him in such terms. His idea of it was that he had been making a fool of himself, running around like a chicken with its head cut off—such was the simile that occurred to him. Well, he was bound to freeze anyway, and he might as well take it decently. With this new-found peace of mind came the first glimmerings of drowsiness. A good idea, he thought, to sleep off to death.

It was like taking an anæsthetic. Freezing was not so bad as people thought. There were lots worse ways to die.

He pictured the boys finding his body next day. Suddenly he found himself with them, coming along the trail and looking for himself. And, still with them, he came around a turn in the trail and found himself lying in the snow. He did not belong with himself any more, for even then he was out of himself, standing with the boys and looking at himself in the snow. It certainly was cold, was his thought. When he got back to the States he could tell the folks what real cold was. He drifted on from this to a vision of the old-timer on Sulphur Creek. He could see him quite clearly, warm and comfortable, and smoking a pipe.

"You were right, old hoss; you were right," the man mumbled to the old-timer of Sulphur Creek.

Then the man drowsed off into what seemed to him the most comfortable and satisfying sleep he had ever known. The dog sat facing him and waiting. The brief day drew to a close in a long, slow twilight. There were no signs of a fire to be made, and, besides, never in the dog's experience had it known a man to sit like that in the snow and make no fire. As the twilight drew on, its eager yearning for the fire mastered it, and with a great lifting and shifting of forefeet, it whined softly, then flattened its ears down in anticipation of being chidden by the man. But the man remained silent. Later, the dog whined loudly. And still later it crept close to the man and caught the scent of death. This made the animal bristle and back away. A little longer it delayed, howling under the stars that leaped and danced and shone brightly in the cold sky. Then it turned and trotted up the trail in the direction of the camp it knew, where were the other food-providers and fire-providers.

## THE WIT OF PORPORTUK

EL-SOO had been a Mission girl. Her mother had died when she was very small, and Sister Alberta had plucked El-Soo as a brand from the burning, one summer day, and carried her away to Holy Cross Mission and dedicated her to God. El-Soo was a full-blooded Indian, yet she exceeded all the half-breed and quarter-breed girls. Never had the good sisters dealt with a girl so adaptable and at the same time so spirited.

El-Soo was quick, and deft, and intelligent; but above all she was fire, the living flame of life, a blaze of personality that was compounded of will, sweetness, and daring. Her father was a chief, and his blood ran in her veins. Obedience, on the part of El-Soo, was a matter of terms and arrangement. She had a passion for equity, and perhaps it was because of this that she excelled in mathematics.

But she excelled in other things. She learned to read and write English as no girl had ever learned in the Mission. She led the girls in singing, and into song she carried her sense of equity. She was an artist, and the fire of her flowed toward creation. Had she from birth enjoyed a more favorable environment, she would have made literature or music.

Instead, she was El-Soo, daughter of Klakee-Nah, a chief, and she lived in the Holy Cross Mission where were no artists, but only pure-souled Sisters who were interested in cleanliness and righteousness and the welfare of the spirit in the land of immortality that lay beyond the skies.

The years passed. She was eight years old when she entered the Mission; she was sixteen, and the Sisters were corresponding with their superiors in the Order concerning the sending of El-Soo to the United States to complete her education, when a man of her own tribe arrived at Holy Cross and had talk with her. El-Soo was somewhat appalled by him. He was dirty. He was a Caliban-like creature, primitively ugly, with a mop of hair that had never been combed. He looked at her disapprovingly and refused to sit down.

"Thy brother is dead," he said shortly.

El-Soo was not particularly shocked. She remembered little of her brother. "Thy father is an old man, and alone," the messenger went on. "His house is large and empty, and he would hear thy voice and look upon thee."

Him she remembered—Klakee-Nah, the headman of the village, the friend of the missionaries and the traders, a large man thewed like a giant, with kindly eyes and masterful ways, and striding with a consciousness of crude royalty in his carriage.

"Tell him that I will come," was El-Soo's answer.

Much to the despair of the Sisters, the brand plucked from the burning went back to the burning. All pleading with El-Soo was vain. There was much argument, expostulation, and weeping. Sister Alberta even revealed to her the project of sending her to the United States. El-Soo stared wide-eyed into the golden vista thus opened up to her, and shook her head. In her eyes persisted another vista. It was the mighty curve of the Yukon at Tana-naw Station. With the St. George Mission on one side, and the trading post on the other, and midway between the Indian village and a certain large log house where lived an old man tended upon by slaves.

All dwellers on the Yukon bank for twice a thousand miles knew the large log house, the old man and the tending slaves; and well did the Sisters know the house, its unending revelry, its feasting and its fun. So there was weeping at Holy Cross when El-Soo departed.

There was a great cleaning up in the large house when El-Soo arrived. Klakee-Nah, himself masterful, protested at this masterful conduct of his young daughter; but in the end, dreaming barbarically of magnificence, he went forth and borrowed a thousand dollars from old Porportuk, than whom there was no richer Indian on the Yukon. Also, Klakee-Nah ran up a heavy bill at the trading post. El-Soo re-created the large house. She invested it with new splendor, while Klakee-Nah maintained its ancient traditions of hospitality and revelry.

All this was unusual for a Yukon Indian, but Klakee-Nah was an unusual Indian. Not alone did he like to render inordinate hospitality, but, what of being a chief and of acquiring much money, he was able to do it. In the primitive trading days he had been a power over his people, and he had dealt profitably with the white trading companies. Later on, with Porportuk, he had made a gold-strike on the Koyokuk River. Klakee-Nah was by training and nature an aristocrat. Porportuk was bourgeois, and Porportuk bought him out of the gold-mine. Porportuk was content to plod and accumulate. Klakee-Nah went back to his large house and proceeded to spend. Porportuk was known as the richest Indian in Alaska. Klakee-Nah was known as the whitest. Porportuk was a money-lender and a usurer. Klakee-Nah was an anachronism—a mediæval ruin, a fighter and a feaster, happy with wine and song.

El-Soo adapted herself to the large house and its ways as readily as she had adapted herself to Holy Cross

Mission and its ways. She did not try to reform her father and direct his footsteps toward God. It is true, she reproved him when he drank overmuch and profoundly, but that was for the sake of his health and the direction of his footsteps on solid earth.

The latchstring to the large house was always out. What with the coming and the going, it was never still. The rafters of the great living-room shook with the roar of wassail and of song. At table sat men from all the world and chiefs from distant tribes—Englishmen and Colonials, lean Yankee traders and rotund officials of the great companies, cowboys from the Western ranges, sailors from the sea, hunters and dog-mushers of a score of nationalities.

El-Soo drew breath in a cosmopolitan atmosphere. She could speak English as well as she could her native tongue, and she sang English songs and ballads. The passing Indian ceremonials she knew, and the perishing traditions. The tribal dress of the daughter of a chief she knew how to wear upon occasion. But for the most part she dressed as white women dress. Not for nothing was her needlework at the Mission and her innate artistry. She carried her clothes like a white woman, and she made clothes that could be so carried.

In her way she was as unusual as her father, and the position she occupied was as unique as his. She was the one Indian woman who was the social equal with the several white women at Tana-naw Station. She was the one Indian woman to whom white men honourably made proposals of marriage. And she was the one Indian woman whom no white man ever insulted.

For El-Soo was beautiful—not as white women are beautiful, not as Indian women are beautiful. It was the flame of her, that did not depend upon feature, that was her beauty. So far as mere line and feature went, she was the classic Indian type. The black hair and the fine bronze were hers, and the black eyes, brilliant and bold, keen as sword-light, proud; and hers the delicate eagle nose with the thin, quivering nostrils, the high cheekbones that were not broad apart, and the thin lips that were not too thin. But over all and through all poured the flame of her—the unanalyzable something that was fire and that was the soul of her, that lay mellow-warm or blazed in her eyes, that sprayed the cheeks of her, that distended the nostrils, that curled the lips, or, when the lip was in repose, that was still there in the lip, the lip palpitant with its presence.

And El-Soo had wit—rarely sharp to hurt, yet quick to search out forgivable weakness. The laughter of her mind played like lambent flame over all about her, and from all about her arose answering laughter. Yet she was never the centre of things. This she would not permit. The large house, and all of which it was significant, was her father's; and through it, to the last, moved his heroic figure—host, master of the revels, and giver of the law. It is true, as the strength oozed from him, that she caught up responsibilities from his failing hands. But in appearance he still ruled, dozing, ofttimes at the board, a bacchanalian ruin, yet in all seeming the ruler of the feast.

And through the large house moved the figure of Porportuk, ominous, with shaking head, coldly disapproving, paying for it all. Not that he really paid, for he compounded interest in weird ways, and year by year absorbed the properties of Klakee-Nah. Porportuk once took it upon himself to chide El-Soo upon the wasteful way of life in the large house—it was when he had about absorbed the last of Klakee-Nah's wealth—but he never ventured so to chide again. El-Soo, like her father, was an aristocrat, as disdainful of money as he, and with an equal sense of honour as finely strung.

Porportuk continued grudgingly to advance money, and ever the money flowed in golden foam away. Upon one thing El-Soo was resolved—her father should die as he had lived. There should be for him no passing from high to low, no diminution of the revels, no lessening of the lavish hospitality. When there was famine, as of old, the Indians came groaning to the large house and went away content. When there was famine and no money, money was borrowed from Porportuk, and the Indians still went away content. El-Soo might well have repeated, after the aristocrats of another time and place, that after her came the deluge. In her case the deluge was old Porportuk. With every advance of money, he looked upon her with a more possessive eye, and felt bourgeoning within him ancient fires.

But El-Soo had no eyes for him. Nor had she eyes for the white men who wanted to marry her at the Mission with ring and priest and book. For at Tana-naw Station was a young man, Akoon, of her own blood, and tribe, and village. He was strong and beautiful to her eyes, a great hunter, and, in that he had wandered far and much, very poor; he had been to all the unknown wastes and places; he had journeyed to Sitka and to the United States; he had crossed the continent to Hudson Bay and back again, and as seal-hunter on a ship he had sailed to Siberia and for Japan.

When he returned from the gold-strike in Klondike he came, as was his wont, to the large house to make report to old Klakee-Nah of all the world that he had seen; and there he first saw El-Soo, three years back from the

Mission. Thereat, Akoon wandered no more. He refused a wage of twenty dollars a day as pilot on the big steamboats. He hunted some and fished some, but never far from Tana-naw Station, and he was at the large house often and long. And El-Soo measured him against many men and found him good. He sang songs to her, and was ardent and glowed until all Tana-naw Station knew he loved her. And Porportuk but grinned and advanced more money for the upkeep of the large house.

Then came the death table of Klakee-Nah.

He sat at feast, with death in his throat, that he could not drown with wine. And laughter and joke and song went around, and Akoon told a story that made the rafters echo. There were no tears or sighs at that table. It was no more than fit that Klakee-Nah should die as he had lived, and none knew this better than El-Soo, with her artist sympathy. The old roystering crowd was there, and, as of old, three frost-bitten sailors were there, fresh from the long traverse from the Arctic, survivors of a ship's company of seventy-four. At Klakee-Nah's back were four old men, all that were left him of the slaves of his youth. With rheumy eyes they saw to his needs, with palsied hands filling his glass or striking him on the back between the shoulders when death stirred and he coughed and gasped.

It was a wild night, and as the hours passed and the fun laughed and roared along, death stirred more restlessly in Klakee-Nah's throat. Then it was that he sent for Porportuk. And Porportuk came in from the outside frost to look with disapproving eyes upon the meat and wine on the table for which he had paid. But as he looked down the length of flushed faces to the far end and saw the face of El-Soo, the light in his eyes flared up, and for a moment the disapproval vanished.

Place was made for him at Klakee-Nah's side, and a glass placed before him. Klakee-Nah, with his own hands, filled the glass with fervent spirits. "Drink!" he cried. "Is it not good?"

And Porportuk's eyes watered as he nodded his head and smacked his lips.

"When, in your own house, have you had such drink?" Klakee-Nah demanded.

"I will not deny that the drink is good to this old throat of mine," Porportuk made answer, and hesitated for the speech to complete the thought.

"But it costs overmuch," Klakee-Nah roared, completing it for him.

Porportuk winced at the laughter that went down the table. His eyes burned malevolently. "We were boys together, of the same age," he said. "In your throat is death. I am still alive and strong."

An ominous murmur arose from the company. Klakee-Nah coughed and strangled, and the old slaves smote him between the shoulders. He emerged gasping, and waved his hand to still the threatening rumble.

"You have grudged the very fire in your house because the wood cost overmuch!" he cried. "You have grudged life. To live cost overmuch, and you have refused to pay the price. Your life has been like a cabin where the fire is out and there are no blankets on the floor." He signalled to a slave to fill his glass, which he held aloft. "But I have lived. And I have been warm with life as you have never been warm. It is true, you shall live long. But the longest nights are the cold nights when a man shivers and lies awake. My nights have been short, but I have slept warm."

He drained the glass. The shaking hand of a slave failed to catch it as it crashed to the floor. Klakee-Nah sank back, panting, watching the upturned glasses at the lips of the drinkers, his own lips slightly smiling to the applause. At a sign, two slaves attempted to help him sit upright again. But they were weak, his frame was mighty, and the four old men tottered and shook as they helped him forward.

"But manner of life is neither here nor there," he went on. "We have other business, Porportuk, you and I, to-night. Debts are mischances, and I am in mischance with you. What of my debt, and how great is it?"

Porportuk searched in his pouch and brought forth a memorandum. He sipped at his glass and began. "There is the note of August, 1889, for three hundred dollars. The interest has never been paid. And the note of the next year for five hundred dollars. This note was included in the note of two months later for a thousand dollars. Then there is the note—"

"Never mind the many notes!" Klakee-Nah cried out impatiently. "They make my head go around and all the things inside my head. The whole! The round whole! How much is it?"

Porportuk referred to his memorandum. "Fifteen thousand nine hundred and sixty-seven dollars and seventy-five cents," he read with careful precision.

"Make it sixteen thousand, make it sixteen thousand," Klakee-Nah said grandly. "Odd numbers were ever a worry. And now—and it is for this that I have sent for you—make me out a new note for sixteen thousand, which I shall sign. I have no thought of the interest. Make it as large as you will, and make it payable in the next world, when I shall meet you by the fire of the Great Father of all Indians. Then the note will be paid. This I promise you. It is the word of Klakee-Nah."

Porportuk looked perplexed, and loudly the laughter arose and shook the room. Klakee-Nah raised his hands. "Nay," he cried. "It is not a joke. I but speak in fairness. It was for this I sent for you, Porportuk. Make out the note."

"I have no dealings with the next world," Porportuk made answer slowly.

"Have you no thought to meet me before the Great Father!" Klakee-Nah demanded. Then he added, "I shall surely be there."

"I have no dealings with the next world," Porportuk repeated sourly.

The dying man regarded him with frank amazement.

"I know naught of the next world," Porportuk explained. "I do business in this world."

Klakee-Nah's face cleared. "This comes of sleeping cold of nights," he laughed. He pondered for a space, then said, "It is in this world that you must be paid. There remains to me this house. Take it, and burn the debt in the candle there."

"It is an old house and not worth the money," Porportuk made answer.

"There are my mines on the Twisted Salmon."

"They have never paid to work," was the reply.

"There is my share in the steamer *Koyokuk*. I am half owner."

"She is at the bottom of the Yukon."

Klakee-Nah started. "True, I forgot. It was last spring when the ice went out." He mused for a time while the glasses remained untasted, and all the company waited upon his utterance.

"Then it would seem I owe you a sum of money which I cannot pay . . . in this world?" Porportuk nodded and glanced down the table.

"Then it would seem that you, Porportuk, are a poor business man," Klakee-Nah said slyly. And boldly Porportuk made answer, "No; there is security yet untouched."

"What!" cried Klakee-Nah. "Have I still property? Name it, and it is yours, and the debt is no more."

"There it is." Porportuk pointed at El-Soo.

Klakee-Nah could not understand. He peered down the table, brushed his eyes, and peered again.

"Your daughter, El-Soo—her will I take and the debt be no more. I will burn the debt there in the candle."

Klakee-Nah's great chest began to heave. "Ho! ho!—a joke. Ho! ho! ho!" he laughed Homerically. "And with your cold bed and daughters old enough to be the mother of El-Soo! Ho! ho! ho!" He began to cough and strangle, and the old slaves smote him on the back. "Ho! ho!" he began again, and went off into another paroxysm.

Porportuk waited patiently, sipping from his glass and studying the double row of faces down the board. "It is no joke," he said finally. "My speech is well meant."

Klakee-Nah sobered and looked at him, then reached for his glass, but could not touch it. A slave passed it to him, and glass and liquor he flung into the face of Porportuk.

"Turn him out!" Klakee-Nah thundered to the waiting table that strained like a pack of hounds in leash. "And roll him in the snow!"

As the mad riot swept past him and out of doors, he signalled to the slaves, and the four tottering old men supported him on his feet as he met the returning revellers, upright, glass in hand, pledging them a toast to the short night when a man sleeps warm.

It did not take long to settle the estate of Klakee-Nah. Tommy, the little Englishman, clerk at the trading post, was called in by El-Soo to help. There was nothing but debts, notes overdue, mortgaged properties, and properties mortgaged but worthless. Notes and mortgages were held by Porportuk. Tommy called him a robber many times as he pondered the compounding of the interest.

"Is it a debt, Tommy?" El-Soo asked.

"It is a robbery," Tommy answered.

"Nevertheless, it is a debt," she persisted.

The winter wore away, and the early spring, and still the claims of Porportuk remained unpaid. He saw El-Soo often and explained to her at length, as he had explained to her father, the way the debt could be cancelled. Also, he brought with him old medicine-men, who elaborated to her the everlasting damnation of her father if the debt were not paid. One day, after such an elaboration, El-Soo made final announcement to Porportuk.

"I shall tell you two things," she said. "First I shall not be your wife. Will you remember that? Second, you shall be paid the last cent of the sixteen thousand dollars—"

"Fifteen thousand nine hundred and sixty-seven dollars and seventy-five cents," Porportuk corrected.

"My father said sixteen thousand," was her reply. "You shall be paid."

"How?"

"I know not how, but I shall find out how. Now go, and bother me no more. If you do"—she hesitated to find fitting penalty—"if you do, I shall have you rolled in the snow again as soon as the first snow flies."

This was still in the early spring, and a little later El-Soo surprised the country. Word went up and down the Yukon from Chilcoot to the Delta, and was carried from camp to camp to the farthermost camps, that in June, when the first salmon ran, El-Soo, daughter of

Klakee-Nah, would sell herself at public auction to satisfy the claims of Porportuk. Vain were the attempts to dissuade her. The missionary at St. George wrestled with her, but she replied—

"Only the debts to God are settled in the next world. The debts of men are of this world, and in this world are they settled."

Akoon wrestled with her, but she replied, "I do love thee, Akoon; but honour is greater than love, and who am I that I should blacken my father?" Sister Alberta journeyed all the way up from Holy Cross on the first steamer, and to no better end.

"My father wanders in the thick and endless forests," said El-Soo. "And there will he wander, with the lost souls crying, till the debt be paid. Then, and not until then, may he go on to the house of the Great Father."

"And you believe this?" Sister Alberta asked.

"I do not know," El-Soo made answer. "It was my father's belief."

Sister Alberta shrugged her shoulders incredulously.

"Who knows but that the things we believe come true?" El-Soo went on. "Why not? The next world to you may be heaven and harps . . . because you have believed heaven and harps; to my father the next world may be a large house where he will sit always at table feasting with God."

"And you?" Sister Alberta asked. "What is your next world?"

El-Soo hesitated but for a moment. "I should like a little of both," she said. "I should like to see your face as well as the face of my father."

The day of the auction came. Tana-naw Station was populous. As was their custom, the tribes had gathered to await the salmon-run, and in the meantime spent the time in dancing and frolicking, trading and gossiping. Then there was the ordinary sprinkling of white adventurers, traders, and prospectors, and, in addition, a large number of white men who had come because of curiosity or interest in the affair.

It had been a backward spring, and the salmon were late in running. This delay but keyed up the interest. Then, on the day of the auction, the situation was made tense by Akoon. He arose and made public and solemn announcement that whosoever bought El-Soo would forthwith and immediately die. He flourished the Winchester in his hand to indicate the manner of the taking-off. El-Soo was angered thereat; but he refused to speak with her, and went to the trading post to lay in extra ammunition.

The first salmon was caught at ten o'clock in the evening, and at midnight the auction began. It took place on top of the high bank alongside the Yukon. The sun was due north just below the horizon, and the sky was lurid red. A great crowd gathered about the table and the two chairs that stood near the edge of the bank. To the fore were many white men and several chiefs. And most prominently to the fore, rifle in hand, stood Akoon. Tommy, at El-Soo's request, served as auctioneer, but she made the opening speech and described the goods about to be sold. She was in native costume, in the dress of a chief's daughter, splendid and barbaric, and she stood on a chair, that she might be seen to advantage.

"Who will buy a wife?" she asked. "Look at me. I am twenty years old and a maid. I will be a good wife to the man who buys me. If he is a white man, I shall dress in the fashion of white women; if he is an Indian, I shall dress as"—she hesitated a moment—"a squaw. I can make my own clothes, and sew, and wash, and mend. I was taught for eight years to do these things at Holy Cross Mission. I can read and write English, and I know how to play the organ. Also I can do arithmetic and some algebra—a little. I shall be sold to the highest bidder, and to him I will make out a bill of sale of myself. I forgot to say that I can sing very well, and that I have never been sick in my life. I weigh one hundred and thirty-two pounds; my father is dead and I have no relatives. Who wants me?"

She looked over the crowd with flaming audacity and stepped down. At Tommy's request she stood upon the chair again, while he mounted the second chair and started the bidding.

Surrounding El-Soo stood the four old slaves of her father. They were age-twisted and palsied, faithful to their meat, a generation out of the past that watched unmoved the antics of younger life. In the front of the crowd were several Eldorado and Bonanza kings from the Upper Yukon, and beside them, on crutches, swollen with scurvy, were two broken prospectors. From the midst of the crowd, thrust out by its own vividness, appeared the face of a wild-eyed squaw from the remote regions of the Upper Tana-naw; a strayed Sitkan from the coast stood side by side with a Stick from Lake Le Barge, and, beyond, a half-dozen French-Canadian voyageurs, grouped by themselves. From afar came the faint cries of myriads of wild-fowl on the nesting-grounds. Swallows were skimming up overhead from the placid surface of the Yukon, and robins were singing. The oblique rays of the hidden sun shot through the smoke, high-dissipated from forest fires a thousand miles away, and turned the heavens to sombre red, while the earth shone red in the reflected glow. This red glow shone in the faces of all, and made everything seem unearthly and unreal.

The bidding began slowly. The Sitkan, who was a stranger in the land and who had arrived only half an hour before, offered one hundred dollars in a confident voice, and was surprised when Akoon turned threateningly upon him with the rifle. The bidding dragged. An Indian from the Tozikakat, a pilot, bid one hundred and fifty, and after some time a gambler, who had been ordered out of the Upper Country, raised the bid to two hundred. El-Soo was saddened; her pride was hurt; but the only effect was that she flamed more audaciously upon the crowd.

There was a disturbance among the onlookers as Porportuk forced his way to the front. "Five hundred dollars!" he bid in a loud voice, then looked about him proudly to note the effect.

He was minded to use his great wealth as a bludgeon with which to stun all competition at the start. But one of the voyageurs, looking on El-Soo with sparkling eyes, raised the bid a hundred.

"Seven hundred!" Porportuk returned promptly.

And with equal promptness came the "Eight hundred" of the voyageur.

Then Porportuk swung his club again.

"Twelve hundred!" he shouted.

With a look of poignant disappointment, the voyageur succumbed. There was no further bidding. Tommy worked hard, but could not elicit a bid.

El-Soo spoke to Porportuk. "It were good, Porportuk, for you to weigh well your bid. Have you forgotten the thing I told you—that I would never marry you!"

"It is a public auction," he retorted. "I shall buy you with a bill of sale. I have offered twelve hundred dollars. You come cheap."

"Too damned cheap!" Tommy cried. "What if I am auctioneer? That does not prevent me from bidding. I'll make it thirteen hundred."

"Fourteen hundred," from Porportuk.

"I'll buy you in to be my—my sister," Tommy whispered to El-Soo, then called aloud, "Fifteen hundred!"

At two thousand one of the Eldorado kings took a hand, and Tommy dropped out.

A third time Porportuk swung the club of his wealth, making a clean raise of five hundred dollars. But the Eldorado king's pride was touched. No man could club him. And he swung back another five hundred.

El-Soo stood at three thousand. Porportuk made it thirty-five hundred, and gasped when the Eldorado king raised it a thousand dollars. Porportuk again raised it five hundred, and again gasped when the king raised a thousand more.

Porportuk became angry. His pride was touched; his strength was challenged, and with him strength took the form of wealth. He would not be ashamed for weakness before the world. El-Soo became incidental. The savings and scrimpings from the cold nights of all his years were ripe to be squandered. El-Soo stood at six thousand. He made it seven thousand. And then, in thousand-dollar bids, as fast as they could be uttered, her price went up. At fourteen thousand the two men stopped for breath.

Then the unexpected happened. A still heavier club was swung. In the pause that ensued, the gambler, who had scented a speculation and formed a syndicate with several of his fellows, bid sixteen thousand dollars.

"Seventeen thousand," Porportuk said weakly.

"Eighteen thousand," said the king.

Porportuk gathered his strength. "Twenty thousand."

The syndicate dropped out. The Eldorado king raised a thousand, and Porportuk raised back; and as they bid, Akoon turned from one to the other, half menacingly, half curiously, as though to see what manner of man it was that he would have to kill. When the king prepared to make his next bid, Akoon having pressed closer, the king first loosed the revolver at his hip, then said:

"Twenty-three thousand."

"Twenty-four thousand," said Porportuk. He grinned viciously, for the certitude of his bidding had at last shaken the king. The latter moved over close to El-Soo. He studied her carefully for a long while.

"And five hundred," he said at last.

"Twenty-five thousand," came Porportuk's raise.

The king looked for a long space, and shook his head. He looked again, and said reluctantly, "And five hundred."

"Twenty-six thousand," Porportuk snapped.

The king shook his head and refused to meet Tommy's pleading eye. In the meantime Akoon had edged close to Porportuk. El-Soo's quick eye noted this, and, while Tommy wrestled with the Eldorado king for another bid, she bent, and spoke in a low voice in the ear of a slave. And while Tommy's "Going—going—going—" dominated the air, the slave went up to Akoon and spoke in a low voice in his ear. Akoon made no sign that he had heard, though El-Soo watched him anxiously.

"Gone!" Tommy's voice rang out. "To Porportuk, for twenty-six thousand dollars."

Porportuk glanced uneasily at Akoon. All eyes were centred upon Akoon, but he did nothing.

"Let the scales be brought," said El-Soo.

"I shall make payment at my house," said Porportuk.

"Let the scales be brought," El-Soo repeated. "Payment shall be made here where all can see."

So the gold scales were brought from the trading post, while Porportuk went away and came back with a man at his heels, on whose shoulders was a weight of gold-dust in moose-hide sacks. Also, at Porportuk's back, walked another man with a rifle, who had eyes only for Akoon.

"Here are the notes and mortgages," said Porportuk, "for fifteen thousand nine hundred and sixty-seven dollars and seventy-five cents."

El-Soo received them into her hands and said to Tommy, "Let them be reckoned as sixteen thousand."

"There remains ten thousand dollars to be paid in gold," Tommy said.

Porportuk nodded, and untied the mouths of the sacks. El-Soo, standing at the edge of the bank, tore the papers to shreds and sent them fluttering out over the Yukon. The weighing began, but halted.

"Of course, at seventeen dollars," Porportuk had said to Tommy, as he adjusted the scales.

"At sixteen dollars," El-Soo said sharply.

"It is the custom of all the land to reckon gold at seventeen dollars for each ounce," Porportuk replied. "And this is a business transaction."

El-Soo laughed. "It is a new custom," she said. "It began this spring. Last year, and the years before, it was sixteen dollars an ounce. When my father's debt was made, it was sixteen dollars. When he spent at the store the money he got from you, for one ounce he was given sixteen dollars' worth of flour, not seventeen. Wherefore, shall you pay for me at sixteen, and not at seventeen." Porportuk grunted and allowed the weighing to proceed.

"Weigh it in three piles, Tommy," she said. "A thousand dollars here, three thousand here, and here six thousand."

It was slow work, and, while the weighing went on, Akoon was closely watched by all.

"He but waits till the money is paid," one said; and the word went around and was accepted, and they waited for what Akoon should do when the money was paid. And Porportuk's man with the rifle waited and watched Akoon.

The weighing was finished, and the gold-dust lay on the table in three dark-yellow heaps. "There is a debt of my father to the Company for three thousand dollars," said El-Soo. "Take it, Tommy, for the Company. And here are four old men, Tommy. You know them. And here is one thousand dollars. Take it, and see that the old men are never hungry and never without tobacco."

Tommy scooped the gold into separate sacks. Six thousand dollars remained on the table. El-Soo thrust the scoop into the heap, and with a sudden turn whirled the contents out and down to the Yukon in a golden shower. Porportuk seized her wrist as she thrust the scoop a second time into the heap.

"It is mine," she said calmly. Porportuk released his grip, but he gritted his teeth and scowled darkly as she continued to scoop the gold into the river till none was left.

The crowd had eyes for naught but Akoon, and the rifle of Porportuk's man lay across the hollow of his arm, the muzzle directed at Akoon a yard away, the man's thumb on the hammer. But Akoon did nothing.

"Make out the bill of sale," Porportuk said grimly.

And Tommy made out the till of sale, wherein all right and title in the woman El-Soo was vested in the man Porportuk. El-Soo signed the document, and Porportuk folded it and put it away in his pouch. Suddenly his eyes flashed, and in sudden speech he addressed El-Soo.

"But it was not your father's debt," he said, "What I paid was the price for you. Your sale is business of to-day and not of last year and the years before. The ounces paid for you will buy at the post to-day seventeen dollars of flour, and not sixteen. I have lost a dollar on each ounce. I have lost six hundred and twenty-five dollars."

El-Soo thought for a moment, and saw the error she had made. She smiled, and then she laughed.

"You are right," she laughed, "I made a mistake. But it is too late. You have paid, and the gold is gone. You did not think quick. It is your loss. Your wit is slow these days, Porportuk. You are getting old."

He did not answer. He glanced uneasily at Akoon, and was reassured. His lips tightened, and a hint of cruelty came into his face. "Come," he said, "we will go to my house."

"Do you remember the two things I told you in the spring?" El-Soo asked, making no movement to accompany him.

"My head would be full with the things women say, did I heed them," he answered.

"I told you that you would be paid," El-Soo went on carefully. "And I told you that I would never be your wife."

"But that was before the bill of sale." Porportuk crackled the paper between his fingers inside the pouch. "I have bought you before all the world. You belong to me. You will not deny that you belong to me."

"I belong to you," El-Soo said steadily.

"I own you."

"You own me."

Porportuk's voice rose slightly and triumphantly. "As a dog, I own you."

"As a dog you own me," El-Soo continued calmly. "But, Porportuk, you forget the thing I told you. Had any other man bought me, I should have been that man's wife. I should have been a good wife to that man. Such was my will. But my will with you was that I should never be your wife. Wherefore, I am your dog."

Porportuk knew that he played with fire, and he resolved to play firmly. "Then I speak to you, not as El-Soo, but as a dog," he said; "and I tell you to come with me." He half reached to grip her arm, but with a gesture she held him back.

"Not so fast, Porportuk. You buy a dog. The dog runs away. It is your loss. I am your dog. What if I run away?"

"As the owner of the dog, I shall beat you—"

"When you catch me?"

"When I catch you."

"Then catch me."

He reached swiftly for her, but she eluded him. She laughed as she circled around the table. "Catch her!" Porportuk commanded the Indian with the rifle, who stood near to her. But as the Indian stretched forth his arm to her, the Eldorado king felled him with a fist blow under the ear. The rifle clattered to the ground. Then was Akoon's chance. His eyes glittered, but he did nothing.

Porportuk was an old man, but his cold nights retained for him his activity. He did not circle the table. He came across suddenly, over the top of the table. El-

Soo was taken off her guard. She sprang back with a sharp cry of alarm, and Porportuk would have caught her had it not been for Tommy. Tommy's leg went out, Porportuk tripped and pitched forward on the ground. El-Soo got her start.

"Then catch me," she laughed over her shoulder, as she fled away.

She ran lightly and easily, but Porportuk ran swiftly and savagely. He outran her. In his youth he had been swiftest of all the young men. But El-Soo dodged in a willowy, elusive way. Being in native dress, her feet were not cluttered with skirts, and her pliant body curved a flight that defied the gripping fingers of Porportuk.

With laughter and tumult, the great crowd scattered out to see the chase. It led through the Indian encampment; and ever dodging, circling, and reversing, El-Soo and Porportuk appeared and disappeared among the tents. El-Soo seemed to balance herself against the air with her arms, now one side, now on the other, and sometimes her body, too, leaned out upon the air far from the perpendicular as she achieved her sharpest curves. And Porportuk, always a leap behind, or a leap this side or that, like a lean hound strained after her.

They crossed the open ground beyond the encampment and disappeared in the forest. Tana-naw Station waited their reappearance, and long and vainly it waited.

In the meantime Akoon ate and slept, and lingered much at the steamboat landing, deaf to the rising resentment of Tana-naw Station in that he did nothing. Twenty-four hours later Porportuk returned. He was tired and savage. He spoke to no one but Akoon, and with him tried to pick a quarrel. But Akoon shrugged his shoulders and walked away. Porportuk did not waste time. He outfitted half a dozen of the young men, selecting the best trackers and travellers, and at their head plunged into the forest.

Next day the steamer *Seattle*, bound up river, pulled in to the shore and wooded up. When the lines were cast off and she churned out from the bank, Akoon was on board in the pilot-house. Not many hours afterward, when it was his turn at the wheel, he saw a small birch-bark canoe put off from the shore. There was only one person in it. He studied it carefully, put the wheel over, and slowed down.

The captain entered the pilot-house. "What's the matter?" he demanded. "The water's good."

Akoon grunted. He saw a larger canoe leaving the bank, and in it were a number of persons. As the *Seattle* lost headway, he put the wheel over some more.

The captain fumed. "It's only a squaw," he protested.

Akoon did not grunt. He was all eyes for the squaw and the pursuing canoe. In the latter six paddles were flashing, while the squaw paddled slowly.

"You'll be aground," the captain protested, seizing the wheel.

But Akoon countered his strength on the wheel and looked him in the eyes. The captain slowly released the spokes.

"Queer beggar," he sniffed to himself.

Akoon held the *Seattle* on the edge of the shoal water and waited till he saw the squaw's fingers clutch the forward rail. Then he signalled for full speed ahead and ground the wheel over. The large canoe was very near, but the gap between it and the steamer was widening.

The squaw laughed and leaned over the rail.

"Then catch me, Porportuk!" she cried.

Akoon left the steamer at Fort Yukon. He outfitted a small poling-boat and went up the Porcupine River. And with him went El-Soo. It was a weary journey, and the way led across the backbone of the world; but Akoon had travelled it before. When they came to the head-waters of the Porcupine, they left the boat and went on foot across the Rocky Mountains.

Akoon greatly liked to walk behind El-Soo and watch the movements of her. There was a music in it that he loved. And especially he loved the well-rounded calves in their sheaths of soft-tanned leather, the slim ankles, and the small moccasined feet that were tireless through the longest days.

"You are light as air," he said, looking up at her. "It is no labour for you to walk. You almost float, so lightly do your feet rise and fall. You are like a deer, El-Soo; you are like a deer, and your eyes are like deer's eyes, sometimes when you look at me, or when you hear a quick sound and wonder if it be danger that stirs. Your eyes are like a deer's eyes now as you look at me."

And El-Soo, luminous and melting, bent and kissed Akoon.

"When we reach the Mackenzie, we will not delay," Akoon said later. "We will go south before the winter catches us. We will go to the sunlands where there is no snow. But we will return. I have seen much of the world, and there is no land like Alaska, no sun like our sun, and the snow is good after the long summer."

"And you will learn to read," said El-Soo.

And Akoon said, "I will surely learn to read." But there was delay when they reached the Mackenzie. They fell in with a band of Mackenzie Indians, and, hunting,

Akoon was shot by accident. The rifle was in the hands of a youth. The bullet broke Akoon's right arm and, ranging farther, broke two of his ribs. Akoon knew rough surgery, while El-Soo had learned some refinements at Holy Cross. The bones were finally set, and Akoon lay by the fire for them to knit. Also, he lay by the fire so that the smoke would keep the mosquitoes away.

Then it was that Porportuk, with his six young men, arrived. Akoon groaned in his helplessness and made appeal to the Mackenzies. But Porportuk made demand, and the Mackenzies were perplexed. Porportuk was for seizing upon El-Soo, but this they would not permit. Judgment must be given, and, as it was an affair of man and woman, the council of the old men was called—this that warm judgment might not be given by the young men, who were warm of heart.

The old men sat in a circle about the smudge-fire. Their faces were lean and wrinkled, and they gasped and panted for air. The smoke was not good for them. Occasionally they struck with withered hands at the mosquitoes that braved the smoke. After such exertion they coughed hollowly and painfully. Some spat blood, and one of them sat a bit apart with head bowed forward, and bled slowly and continuously at the mouth; the coughing sickness had gripped them. They were as dead men; their time was short. It was a judgment of the dead.

"And I paid for her a heavy price," Porportuk concluded his complaint. "Such a price you have never seen. Sell all that is yours—sell your spears and arrows and rifles, sell your skins and furs, sell your tents and boats and dogs, sell everything, and you will not have maybe a thousand dollars. Yet did I pay for the woman, El-Soo, twenty-six times the price of all your spears and arrows and rifles, your skins and furs, your tents and boats and dogs. It was a heavy price."

The old men nodded gravely, though their weazened eye-slits widened with wonder that any woman should be worth such a price. The one that bled at the mouth wiped his lips. "Is it true talk?" he asked each of Porportuk's six young men. And each answered that it was true.

"Is it true talk?" he asked El-Soo, and she answered, "It is true."

"But Porportuk has not told that he is an old man," Akoon said, "and that he has daughters older than El-Soo."

"It is true, Porportuk is an old man," said El-Soo.

"It is for Porportuk to measure the strength his age," said he who bled at the mouth. "We be old men. Behold! Age is never so old as youth would measure it."

And the circle of old men champed their gums, and nodded approvingly, and coughed.

"I told him that I would never be his wife," said El-Soo.

"Yet you took from him twenty-six times all that we possess?" asked a one-eyed old man.

El-Soo was silent.

"It is true?" And his one eye burned and bored into her like a fiery gimlet.

"It is true," she said.

"But I will run away again," she broke out passionately, a moment later. "Always will I run away."

"That is for Porportuk to consider," said another of the old men. "It is for us to consider the judgment."

"What price did you pay for her?" was demanded of Akoon.

"No price did I pay for her," he answered. "She was above price. I did not measure her in gold-dust, nor in dogs, and tents, and furs."

The old men debated among themselves and mumbled in undertones. "These old men are ice," Akoon said in English. "I will not listen to their judgment, Porportuk. If you take El-Soo, I will surely kill you."

The old men ceased and regarded him suspiciously. "We do not know the speech you make," one said.

"He but said that he would kill me," Porportuk volunteered. "So it were well to take from him his rifle, and to have some of your young men sit by him, that he may not do me hurt. He is a young man, and what are broken bones to youth!"

Akoon, lying helpless, had rifle and knife taken from him, and to either side of his shoulders sat young men of the Mackenzies. The one-eyed old man arose and stood upright. "We marvel at the price paid for one mere woman," he began; "but the wisdom of the price is no concern of ours. We are here to give judgment, and judgment we give. We have no doubt. It is known to all that Porportuk paid a heavy price for the woman El-Soo. Wherefore does the woman El-Soo belong to Porportuk and none other." He sat down heavily, and coughed. The old men nodded and coughed.

"I will kill you," Akoon cried in English.

Porportuk smiled and stood up. "You have given true judgment," he said to the council, "and my young men will give to you much tobacco. Now let the woman be brought to me."

Akoon gritted his teeth. The young men took El-Soo by the arms. She did not resist, and was led, her face a sullen flame, to Porportuk.

"Sit there at my feet till I have made my talk," he commanded. He paused a moment. "It is true," he said, "I am an old man. Yet can I understand the ways of youth. The fire has not all gone out of me. Yet am I no longer young, nor am I minded to run these old legs of mine through all the years that remain to me. El-Soo can run fast and well. She is a deer. This I know, for I have seen and run after her. It is not good that a wife should run so fast. I paid for her a heavy price, yet does she run away from me. Akoon paid no price at all, yet does she run to him.

"When I came among you people of the Mackenzie, I was of one mind. As I listened in the council and thought of the swift legs of El-Soo, I was of many minds. Now am I of one mind again but it is a different mind from the one I brought to the council. Let me tell you my mind. When a dog runs once away from a master, it will run away again. No matter how many times it is brought back, each time it will run away again. When we have such dogs, we sell them. El-Soo is like a dog that runs away. I will sell her. Is there any man of the council that will buy?"

The old men coughed and remained silent

"Akoon would buy," Porportuk went on, "but he has no money. Wherefore I will give El-Soo to him, as he said, without price. Even now will I give her to him."

Reaching down, he took El-Soo by the hand and led her across the space to where Akoon lay on his back.

"She has a bad habit, Akoon," he said, seating her at Akoon's feet. "As she has run away from me in the past, in the days to come she may run away from you. But there is no need to fear that she will ever run away, Akoon. I shall see to that. Never will she run away from you—this is the word of Porportuk. She has great wit. I know, for often has it bitten into me. Yet am I minded myself to give my wit play for once. And by my wit will I secure her to you, Akoon."

Stooping, Porportuk crossed El-Soo's feet, so that the instep of one lay over that of the other; and then, before his purpose could be divined, he discharged his rifle through the two ankles. As Akoon struggled to rise against the weight of the young men, there was heard the crunch of the broken bone rebroken.

"It is just," said the old men, one to another.

El-Soo made no sound. She sat and looked at her shattered ankles, on which she would never walk again.

"My legs are strong, El-Soo," Akoon said. "But never will they bear me away from you."

El-Soo looked at him, and for the first time in all the time he had known her, Akoon saw tears in her eyes.

"Your eyes are like deer's eyes, El-Soo," he said.

"Is it just?" Porportuk asked, and grinned from the edge of the smoke as he prepared to depart.

"It is just," the old men said. And they sat on in the silence.

## THE WHITE SILENCE

"CARMEN won't last more than a couple of days." Mason spat out a chunk of ice and surveyed the poor animal ruefully, then put her foot in his mouth and proceeded to bite out the ice which clustered cruelly between the toes.

"I never saw a dog with a highfalutin' name that ever was worth a rap," he said, as he concluded his task and shoved her aside. "They just fade away and die under the responsibility. Did ye ever see one go wrong with a sensible name like Cassiar, Siwash, or Husky? No, sir! Take a look at Shookum here, he's"—

Snap! The lean brute flashed up, the white teeth just missing Mason's throat.

"Ye will, will ye?" A shrewd clout behind the ear with the butt of the dog whip stretched the animal in the snow, quivering softly, a yellow slaver dripping from its fangs.

"As I was saying, just look at Shookum here—he's got the spirit. Bet ye he eats Carmen before the week's out."

"I'll bank another proposition against that," replied Malemute Kid, reversing the frozen bread placed before the fire to thaw. "We'll eat Shookum before the trip is over. What d'ye say, Ruth?"

The Indian woman settled the coffee with a piece of ice, glanced from Malemute Kid to her husband, then at the dogs, but vouchsafed no reply. It was such a palpable truism that none was necessary. Two hundred miles of unbroken trail in prospect, with a scant six days' grub for themselves and none for the dogs, could admit no other alternative. The two men and the woman grouped about the fire and began their meager meal. The dogs lay in their harnesses for it was a midday halt, and watched each mouthful enviously.

"No more lunches after today," said Malemute Kid. "And we've got to keep a close eye on the dogs—they're getting vicious. They'd just as soon pull a fellow down as not, if they get a chance."

"And I was president of an Epworth once, and taught in the Sunday school." Having irrelevantly delivered himself of this, Mason fell into a dreamy contemplation of his steaming moccasins, but was aroused by Ruth filling his cup. "Thank God, we've got slathers of tea! I've seen it growing, down in Tennessee. What wouldn't I give for a hot corn pone just now! Never mind, Ruth; you won't starve much longer, nor wear moccasins either."

The woman threw off her gloom at this, and in her eyes welled up a great love for her white lord—the first white man she had ever seen—the first man whom she had known to treat a woman as something better than a mere animal or beast of burden.

"Yes, Ruth," continued her husband, having recourse to the macaronic jargon in which it was alone possible for them to understand each other; "wait till we clean up and pull for the Outside. We'll take the White Man's canoe and go to the Salt Water. Yes, bad water, rough water—great mountains dance up and down all the time. And so big, so far, so far away—you travel ten sleep, twenty sleep, forty sleep"—he graphically enumerated the days on his fingers—"all the time water, bad water. Then you come to great village, plenty people, just the same mosquitoes next summer. Wigwams oh, so high—ten, twenty pines. Hi-yu skookum!"

He paused impotently, cast an appealing glance at Malemute Kid, then laboriously placed the twenty pines, end on end, by sign language. Malemute Kid smiled with cheery cynicism; but Ruth's eyes were wide with wonder, and with pleasure; for she half believed he was joking, and such condescension pleased her poor woman's heart.

"And then you step into a—a box, and pouf! up you go." He tossed his empty cup in the air by way of illustration and, as he deftly caught it, cried: "And biff! down you come. Oh, great medicine men! You go Fort Yukon. I go Arctic City—twenty-five sleep—big string, all the time—I catch him string—I say, 'Hello, Ruth! How are ye?'—and you say, 'Is that my good husband?'—and I say, 'Yes'—and you say, 'No can bake good bread, no more soda'—then I say, 'Look in cache, under flour; good-by.' You look and catch plenty soda. All the time you Fort Yukon, me Arctic City. Hi-yu medicine man!"

Ruth smiled so ingenuously at the fairy story that both men burst into laughter. A row among the dogs cut short the wonders of the Outside, and by the time the snarling combatants were separated, she had lashed the sleds and all was ready for the trail.

"Mush! Baldy! Hi! Mush on!" Mason worked his whip smartly and, as the dogs whined low in the traces, broke out the sled with the gee pole. Ruth followed with the second team, leaving Malemute Kid, who had helped her start, to bring up the rear. Strong man, brute that he was, capable of felling an ox at a blow, he could not bear to beat the poor animals, but humored them as a dog driver rarely does—nay, almost wept with them in their misery.

"Come, mush on there, you poor sore-footed brutes!" he murmured, after several ineffectual attempts to start the load. But his patience was at last rewarded, and though whimpering with pain, they hastened to join their fellows.

No more conversation; the toil of the trail will not permit such extravagance.

And of all deadening labors, that of the Northland trail is the worst. Happy is the man who can weather a day's travel at the price of silence, and that on a beaten track. And of all heartbreaking labors, that of breaking trail is the worst. At every step the great webbed shoe sinks till the snow is level with the knee. Then up, straight up, the deviation of a fraction of an inch being a certain precursor of disaster, the snowshoe must be lifted till the surface is cleared; then forward, down, and the other foot is raised perpendicularly for the matter of half a yard. He who tries this for the first time, if haply he avoids bringing his shoes in dangerous propinquity and measures not his length on the treacherous footing, will give up exhausted at the end of a hundred yards; he who can keep out of the way of the dogs for a whole day may well crawl into his sleeping bag with a clear conscience and a pride which passeth all understanding; and he who travels twenty sleeps on the Long Trail is a man whom the gods may envy.

The afternoon wore on, and with the awe, born of the White Silence, the voiceless travelers bent to their work. Nature has many tricks wherewith she convinces man of his finity—the ceaseless flow of the tides, the fury of the storm, the shock of the earthquake, the long roll of heaven's artillery—but the most tremendous, the most stupefying of all, is the passive phase of the White Silence.

All movement ceases, the sky clears, the heavens are as brass; the slightest whisper seems sacrilege, and man becomes timid, affrighted at the sound of his own voice. Sole speck of life journeying across the ghostly wastes of a dead world, he trembles at his audacity, realizes that his is a maggot's life, nothing more. Strange thoughts arise unsummoned, and the mystery of all things strives for utterance. And the fear of death, of God, of the universe, comes over him—the hope of the Resurrection and the Life, the yearning for immortality, the vain striving of the imprisoned essence—it is then, if ever, man walks alone with God.

So wore the day away. The river took a great bend, and Mason headed his team for the cutoff across the narrow neck of land. But the dogs balked at the high bank. Again and again, though Ruth and Malemute Kid were shoving on the sled, they slipped back. Then came the concerted effort. The miserable creatures, weak from hunger, exerted their last strength. Up—up—the sled poised on the top of the bank; but the leader swung the string of dogs behind him to the right, fouling Mason's snowshoes. The result was grievous. Mason was whipped off his feet; one of the dogs fell in the traces; and the sled toppled back, dragging everything to the bottom again.

Slash! the whip fell among the dogs savagely, especially upon the one which had fallen.

"Don't, Mason," entreated Malemute Kid; "the poor devil's on its last legs. Wait and We'll put my team on."

Mason deliberately withheld the whip till the last word had fallen, then out flashed the long lash, completely curling about the offending creature's body. Carmen—for it was Carmen—cowered in the snow, cried piteously, then rolled over on her side.

It was a tragic moment, a pitiful incident of the trail—a dying dog, two comrades in anger. Ruth glanced solicitously from man to man. But Malemute Kid restrained himself, though there was a world of reproach in his eyes, and, bending over the dog, cut the traces. No word was spoken. The teams were doublespanned and the difficulty overcome; the sleds were under way again, the dying dog dragging herself along in the rear. As long as an animal can travel, it is not shot, and this last chance is accorded it—the crawling into camp, if it can, in the hope of a moose being killed.

Already penitent for his angry action, but too stubborn to make amends, Mason toiled on at the head of the cavalcade, little dreaming that danger hovered in the air. The timber clustered thick in the sheltered bottom, and through this they threaded their way. Fifty feet or more from the trail towered a lofty pine. For generations it had stood there, and for generations destiny had had this one end in view—perhaps the same had been decreed of Mason.

He stooped to fasten the loosened thong of his moccasin. The sleds came to a halt, and the dogs lay down in the snow without a whimper. The stillness was weird; not a breath rustled the frost-encrusted forest; the cold and silence of outer space had chilled the heart and smote the trembling lips of nature. A sigh pulsed through the air—they did not seem to actually hear it, but rather felt it, like the premonition of movement in a motionless void. Then the great tree, burdened with its weight of years and snow, played its last part in the tragedy of life. He heard the warning crash and attempted to spring up but, almost erect, caught the blow squarely on the shoulder.

The sudden danger, the quick death—how often had Malemute Kid faced it! The pine needles were still quivering as he gave his commands and sprang into action. Nor did the Indian girl faint or raise her voice in idle wailing, as might many of her white sisters. At his order, she threw her weight on the end of a quickly extemporized handspike, easing the pressure and listening to her husband's groans, while Malemute Kid attacked the tree with his ax. The steel rang merrily as it bit into the frozen trunk, each stroke being accompanied by a forced, audible respiration, the "Huh!" "Huh!" of the woodsman.

At last the Kid laid the pitiable thing that was once a man in the snow. But worse than his comrade's pain was the dumb anguish in the woman's face, the blended look of hopeful, hopeless query. Little was said; those of the Northland are early taught the futility of words and the inestimable value of deeds. With the temperature at sixty-five below zero, a man cannot lie many minutes in the snow and live. So the sled lashings were cut, and the sufferer, rolled in furs, laid on a couch of boughs. Before him roared a fire, built of the very wood which wrought the mishap. Behind and partially over him was stretched the primitive fly—a piece of canvas, which caught the radiating heat and threw it back and down upon him—a trick which men may know who study physics at the fount.

And men who have shared their bed with death know when the call is sounded. Mason was terribly crushed. The most cursory examination revealed it. His right arm, leg, and back were broken; his limbs were paralyzed from the hips; and the likelihood of internal injuries was large. An occasional moan was his only sign of life.

No hope; nothing to be done. The pitiless night crept slowly by—Ruth's portion, the despairing stoicism of her race, and Malemute Kid adding new lines to his face of bronze. In fact, Mason suffered least of all, for he spent his time in eastern Tennessee, in the Great Smoky Mountains, living over the scenes of his childhood. And most pathetic was the melody of his long-forgotten Southern vernacular, as he raved of swimming holes and coon hunts and watermelon raids. It was as Greek to Ruth, but the Kid understood and felt—felt as only one can feel who has been shut out for years from all that civilization means.

Morning brought consciousness to the stricken man, and Malemute Kid bent closer to catch his whispers.

"You remember when we foregathered on the Tanana, four years come next ice run? I didn't care so much for her then. It was more like she was pretty, and there was a smack of excitement about it, I think. But d'ye know, I've come to think a heap of her. She's been a good wife to me, always at my shoulder in the pinch. And when it comes to trading, you know there isn't her equal. D'ye recollect the time she shot the Moosehorn Rapids to pull you and me off that rock, the bullets whipping the water like hailstones?—and the time of the famine at Nuklukyeto?—when she raced the ice run to bring the news? Yes, she's been a good wife to me, better'n that other one. Didn't know I'd been there? Never told you, eh? Well, I tried it once, down in the States. That's why I'm here. Been raised together, too. I came away to give her a chance for divorce. She got it.

"But that's got nothing to do with Ruth. I had thought of cleaning up and pulling for the Outside next year—her and I—but it's too late. Don't send her back to her people, Kid. It's beastly hard for a woman to go back. Think of it!—nearly four years on our bacon and beans and flour and dried fruit, and then to go back to her fish and caribou. It's not good for her to have tried our ways, to come to know they're better'n her people's, and then return to them. Take care of her, Kid, why don't you—but no, you always fought shy of them—and you never told me why you came to this country. Be kind to her, and send her back to the States as soon as you can. But fix it so she can come back—liable to get homesick, you know.

"And the youngster—it's drawn us closer, Kid. I only hope it is a boy. Think of it!—flesh of my flesh, Kid. He mustn't stop in this country. And if it's a girl, why, she can't. Sell my furs; they'll fetch at least five thousand, and I've got as much more with the company. And handle my interests with yours. I think that bench claim will show up. See that he gets a good schooling; and Kid, above all, don't let him come back. This country was not made for white men.

"I'm a gone man, Kid. Three or four sleeps at the best. You've got to go on. You must go on! Remember, it's my wife, it's my boy—O God! I hope it's a boy! You can't stay by me—and I charge you, a dying man, to pull on."

"Give me three days," pleaded Malemute Kid. "You may change for the better; something may turn up."

"No."

"Just three days."

"You must pull on."

"Two days."

"It's my wife and my boy, Kid. You would not ask it."

"One day."

"No, no! I charge—"

"Only one day. We can shave it through on the grub, and I might knock over a moose."

"No—all right; one day, but not a minute more. And, Kid, don't—don't leave me to face it alone. Just a shot, one pull on the trigger. You understand. Think of it! Think of it! Flesh of my flesh, and I'll never live to see him!

"Send Ruth here. I want to say good-by and tell her that she must think of the boy and not wait till I'm dead. She might refuse to go with you if I didn't. Goodby, old man; good-by.

"Kid! I say—a—sink a hole above the pup, next to the slide. I panned out forty cents on my shovel there.

"And, Kid!" He stooped lower to catch the last faint words, the dying man's surrender of his pride. "I'm sorry—for—you know—Carmen."

Leaving the girl crying softly over her man, Malemute Kid slipped into his parka and snowshoes, tucked his rifle under his arm, and crept away into the forest. He was no tyro in the stern sorrows of the Northland, but never had he faced so stiff a problem as this. In the abstract, it was a plain, mathematical proposition—three possible lives as against one doomed one. But now he hesitated. For five years, shoulder to shoulder, on the rivers and trails, in the camps and mines, facing death by field and flood and famine, had they knitted the bonds of their comradeship. So close was the tie that he had often been conscious of a vague jealousy of Ruth, from the first time she had come between. And now it must be severed by his own hand.

Though he prayed for a moose, just one moose, all game seemed to have deserted the land, and nightfall found the exhausted man crawling into camp, light-handed, heavyhearted. An uproar from the dogs and shrill cries from Ruth hastened him.

Bursting into the camp, he saw the girl in the midst of the snarling pack, laying about her with an ax. The dogs had broken the iron rule of their masters and were rushing the grub.

He joined the issue with his rifle reversed, and the hoary game of natural selection was played out with all the ruthlessness of its primeval environment. Rifle and ax went up and down, hit or missed with monotonous regularity; lithe bodies flashed, with wild eyes and dripping fangs; and man and beast fought for supremacy to the bitterest conclusion. Then the beaten brutes crept to the edge of the firelight, licking their wounds, voicing their misery to the stars.

The whole stock of dried salmon had been devoured, and perhaps five pounds of flour remained to tide them over two hundred miles of wilderness. Ruth returned to her husband, while Malemute Kid cut up the warm body of one of the dogs, the skull of which had been crushed by the ax. Every portion was carefully put away, save the hide and offal, which were cast to his fellows of the moment before.

Morning brought fresh trouble. The animals were turning on each other. Carmen, who still clung to her slender thread of life, was downed by the pack. The lash fell among them unheeded. They cringed and cried under the blows, but refused to scatter till the last wretched bit had disappeared—bones, hide, hair, everything.

Malemute Kid went about his work, listening to Mason, who was back in Tennessee, delivering tangled discourses and wild exhortations to his brethren of other days.

Taking advantage of neighboring pines, he worked rapidly, and Ruth watched him make a cache similar to those sometimes used by hunters to preserve their meat from the wolverines and dogs. One after the other, he bent the tops of two small pines toward each other and nearly to the ground, making them fast with thongs of moosehide. Then he beat the dogs into submission and harnessed them to two of the sleds, loading the same with everything but the furs which enveloped Mason. These he wrapped and lashed tightly about him, fastening either end of the robes to the bent pines. A single stroke of his hunting knife would release them and send the body high in the air.

Ruth had received her husband's last wishes and made no struggle. Poor girl, she had learned the lesson of obedience well. From a child, she had bowed, and seen all women bow, to the lords of creation, and it did not seem in the nature of things for woman to resist. The Kid permitted her one outburst of grief, as she kissed her husband—her own people had no such custom—then led her to the foremost sled and helped her into her snowshoes. Blindly, instinctively, she took the gee pole and whip, and "mushed" the dogs out on the trail. Then he returned to Mason, who had fallen into a coma, and long after she was out of sight crouched by the fire, waiting, hoping, praying for his comrade to die.

It is not pleasant to be alone with painful thoughts in the White Silence. The silence of gloom is merciful, shrouding one as with protection and breathing a thousand intangible sympathies; but the bright White Silence, clear and cold, under steely skies, is pitiless.

An hour passed—two hours—but the man would not die. At high noon the sun, without raising its rim above the southern horizon, threw a suggestion of fire athwart the heavens, then quickly drew it back. Malemute Kid roused and dragged himself to his comrade's side. He cast one glance about him. The White Silence seemed to sneer, and a great fear came upon him. There was a sharp report; Mason swung into his aerial sepulcher, and Malemute Kid lashed the dogs into a wild gallop as he fled across the snow.

## THE ONE THOUSAND DOZEN

David Rasmunsen was a hustler, and, like many a greater man, a man of the one idea. Wherefore, when the clarion call of the North rang on his ear, he conceived an adventure in eggs and bent all his energy to its achievement. He figured briefly and to the point, and the adventure became iridescent-hued, splendid. That eggs would sell at Dawson for five dollars a dozen was a safe working premise. Whence it was incontrovertible that one thousand dozen would bring, in the Golden Metropolis, five thousand dollars.

On the other hand, expense was to be considered, and he considered it well, for he was a careful man, keenly practical, with a hard head and a heart that imagination never warmed. At fifteen cents a dozen, the initial cost of his thousand dozen would be one hundred and fifty dollars, a mere bagatelle in face of the enormous profit. And suppose, just suppose, to be wildly extravagant for once, that transportation for himself and eggs should run up eight hundred and fifty more; he would still have four thousand clear cash and clean when the last egg was disposed of and the last dust had rippled into his sack.

"You see, Alma,"—he figured it over with his wife, the cosy dining-room submerged in a sea of maps, government surveys, guide-books, and Alaskan itineraries,—"you see, expenses don't really begin till you make Dyea—fifty dollars'll cover it with a first-class passage thrown in. Now from Dyea to Lake Linderman, Indian packers take your goods over for twelve cents a pound, twelve dollars a hundred, or one hundred and twenty dollars a thousand. Say I have fifteen hundred pounds, it'll cost one hundred and eighty dollars—call it two hundred and be safe. I am creditably informed by a Klondiker just come out that I can buy a boat for three hundred. But the same man says I'm sure to get a couple of passengers for one hundred and fifty each, which will give me the boat for nothing, and, further, they can help me manage it. And . . .that's all; I put my eggs ashore from the boat at Dawson. Now let me see how much is that?"

"Fifty dollars from San Francisco to Dyea, two hundred from Dyea to Linderman, passengers pay for the boat—two hundred and fifty all told," she summed up swiftly.

"And a hundred for my clothes and personal outfit," he went on happily; "that leaves a margin of five hundred for emergencies. And what possible emergencies can arise?"

Alma shrugged her shoulders and elevated her brows. If that vast Northland was capable of swallowing up a man and a thousand dozen eggs, surely there was room and to spare for whatever else he might happen to possess. So she thought, but she said nothing. She knew David Rasmunsen too well to say anything.

"Doubling the time because of chance delays, I should make the trip in two months. Think of it, Alma! Four thousand in two months! Beats the paltry hundred a month I'm getting now. Why, we'll build further out where we'll have more space, gas in every room, and a view, and the rent of the cottage'll pay taxes, insurance, and water, and leave something over. And then there's always the chance of my striking it and coming out a millionaire. Now tell me, Alma, don't you think I'm very moderate?"

And Alma could hardly think otherwise. Besides, had not her own cousin,—though a remote and distant one to be sure, the black sheep, the harum-scarum, the ne'er-do-well,—had not he come down out of that weird North country with a hundred thousand in yellow dust, to say nothing of a half-ownership in the hole from which it came?

David Rasmunsen's grocer was surprised when he found him weighing eggs in the scales at the end of the counter, and Rasmunsen himself was more surprised when he found that a dozen eggs weighed a pound and a half—fifteen hundred pounds for his thousand dozen! There would be no weight left for his clothes, blankets, and cooking utensils, to say nothing of the grub he must necessarily consume by the way. His calculations were all thrown out, and he was just proceeding to recast them when he hit upon the idea of weighing small eggs. "For whether they be large or small, a dozen eggs is a dozen eggs," he observed sagely to himself; and a dozen small ones he found to weigh but a pound and a quarter. Thereat the city of San Francisco was overrun by anxious-eyed emissaries, and commission houses and dairy associations were startled by a sudden demand for eggs running not more than twenty ounces to the dozen.

Rasmunsen mortgaged the little cottage for a thousand dollars, arranged for his wife to make a prolonged stay among her own people, threw up his job, and started North. To keep within his schedule he compromised on a second-class passage, which, because of the rush, was worse than steerage; and in the late summer, a pale and wabbly man, he disembarked with his eggs on the Dyea beach. But it did not take him long to recover his land legs and appetite. His first interview with the Chilkoot packers straightened him up and stiffened his backbone. Forty cents a pound they demanded for the twenty-eight-mile portage, and while he caught his breath and swallowed, the price went up to forty-three. Fifteen husky Indians put the straps on his packs at forty-five, but took them off at an offer of forty-seven from a Skaguay Croesus in dirty shirt and ragged overalls who had lost his horses on the White Pass trail and was now making a last desperate drive at the country by way of Chilkoot.

But Rasmunsen was clean grit, and at fifty cents found takers, who, two days later, set his eggs down intact at Linderman. But fifty cents a pound is a thousand dollars a ton, and his fifteen hundred pounds had exhausted his emergency fund and left him stranded at the Tantalus point where each day he saw the fresh-whip-sawed boats departing for Dawson. Further, a great anxiety brooded over the camp where the boats were built. Men worked frantically, early and late, at the height of their endurance, caulking, nailing, and pitching in a frenzy of haste for which adequate explanation was not far to seek. Each day the snow-line crept farther down the bleak, rock-shouldered peaks, and gale followed gale, with sleet and slush and snow, and in the eddies and quiet places young ice formed and thickened through the fleeting hours. And each morn, toil-stiffened men turned wan faces across the lake to see if the freeze-up had come. For the freeze-up heralded the death of their hope—the hope that they would be floating down the swift river ere navigation closed on the chain of lakes.

To harrow Rasmunsen's soul further, he discovered three competitors in the egg business. It was true that one, a little German, had gone broke and was himself forlornly back-tripping the last pack of the portage; but the other two had boats nearly completed, and were daily supplicating the god of merchants and traders to stay the iron hand of winter for just another day. But the iron hand closed down over the land. Men were being frozen in the blizzard which swept Chilkoot, and Rasmunsen frosted his toes ere he was aware. He found a chance to go passenger with his freight in a boat just shoving off through the rubble, but two hundred hard cash, was required, and he had no money.

"Ay tank you yust wait one leedle w'ile," said the Swedish boat-builder, who had struck his Klondike right there and was wise enough to know it—"one leedle w'ile und I make you a tam fine skiff boat, sure Pete."

With this unpledged word to go on, Rasmunsen hit the back trail to Crater Lake, where he fell in with two press correspondents whose tangled baggage was strewn from Stone House, over across the Pass, and as far as Happy Camp.

"Yes," he said with consequence. "I've a thousand dozen eggs at Linderman, and my boat's just about got the last seam caulked. Consider myself in luck to get it. Boats are at a premium, you know, and none to be had."

Whereupon and almost with bodily violence the correspondents clamored to go with him, fluttered greenbacks before his eyes, and spilled yellow twenties from hand to hand. He could not hear of it, but they over-persuaded him, and he reluctantly consented to take them at three hundred apiece. Also they pressed upon him the passage money in advance. And while they wrote to their respective journals concerning the Good Samaritan with the thousand dozen eggs, the Good Samaritan was hurrying back to the Swede at Linderman.

"Here, you! Gimme that boat!" was his salutation, his hand jingling the correspondents' gold pieces and his eyes hungrily bent upon the finished craft.

The Swede regarded him stolidly and shook his head.

"How much is the other fellow paying? Three hundred? Well, here's four. Take it."

He tried to press it upon him, but the man backed away.

"Ay tank not. Ay say him get der skiff boat. You yust wait—"

"Here's six hundred. Last call. Take it or leave it. Tell 'm it's a mistake."

The Swede wavered. "Ay tank yes," he finally said, and the last Rasmunsen saw of him his vocabulary was going to wreck in a vain effort to explain the mistake to the other fellows.

The German slipped and broke his ankle on the steep hogback above Deep Lake, sold out his stock for a dollar a dozen, and with the proceeds hired Indian packers to carry him back to Dyea. But on the morning Rasmunsen shoved off with his correspondents, his two rivals followed suit.

"How many you got?" one of them, a lean little New Englander, called out.

"One thousand dozen," Rasmunsen answered proudly.

"Huh! I'll go you even stakes I beat you in with my eight hundred."

The correspondents offered to lend him the money; but Rasmunsen declined, and the Yankee closed with the remaining rival, a brawny son of the sea and sailor of ships and things, who promised to show them all a wrinkle or two when it came to cracking on. And crack on he did, with a large tarpaulin square-sail which pressed the bow half under at every jump. He was the first to run out of Linderman, but, disdaining the portage, piled his loaded boat on the rocks in the boiling rapids. Rasmunsen and the Yankee, who likewise had two passengers, portaged across on their backs and then lined their empty boats down through the bad water to Bennett.

Bennett was a twenty-five-mile lake, narrow and deep, a funnel between the mountains through which storms ever romped. Rasmunsen camped on the sand-pit at its head, where were many men and boats bound north in the teeth of the Arctic winter. He awoke in the morning to find a piping gale from the south, which caught the chill from the whited peaks and glacial valleys and blew as cold as north wind ever blew. But it was fair, and he also found the Yankee staggering past the first bold headland with all sail set. Boat after boat was getting under way, and the correspondents fell to with enthusiasm.

"We'll catch him before Cariboo Crossing," they assured Rasmunsen, as they ran up the sail and the *Alma* took the first icy spray over her bow.

Now Rasmunsen all his life had been prone to cowardice on water, but he clung to the kicking steering-oar with set face and determined jaw. His thousand dozen were there in the boat before his eyes, safely secured beneath the correspondents' baggage, and somehow, before his eyes were the little cottage and the mortgage for a thousand dollars.

It was bitter cold. Now and again he hauled in the steering-sweep and put out a fresh one while his passengers chopped the ice from the blade. Wherever the spray struck, it turned instantly to frost, and the dipping boom of the spritsail was quickly fringed with icicles. The *Alma* strained and hammered through the big seas till the seams and butts began to spread, but in lieu of bailing the correspondents chopped ice and flung it overboard. There was no let-up. The mad race with winter was on, and the boats tore along in a desperate string.

"W-w-we can't stop to save our souls!" one of the correspondents chattered, from cold, not fright.

"That's right! Keep her down the middle, old man!" the other encouraged.

Rasmunsen replied with an idiotic grin. The iron-bound shores were in a lather of foam, and even down the middle the only hope was to keep running away from the big seas. To lower sail was to be overtaken and swamped. Time and again they passed boats pounding among the rocks, and once they saw one on the edge of the breakers about to strike. A little craft behind them, with two men, jibed over and turned bottom up.

"W-w-watch out, old man," cried he of the chattering teeth.

Rasmunsen grinned and tightened his aching grip on the sweep. Scores of times had the send of the sea caught the big square stern of the *Alma* and thrown her off from dead before it till the after leach of the spritsail fluttered hollowly, and each time, and only with all his strength, had he forced her back. His grin by then had become fixed, and it disturbed the correspondents to look at him.

They roared down past an isolated rock a hundred yards from shore. From its wave-drenched top a man shrieked wildly, for the instant cutting the storm with his voice. But the next instant the *Alma* was by, and the rock growing a black speck in the troubled froth.

"That settles the Yankee! Where's the sailor?" shouted one of his passengers.

Rasmunsen shot a glance over his shoulder at a black square-sail. He had seen it leap up out of the grey to windward, and for an hour, off and on, had been watching it grow. The sailor had evidently repaired damages and was making up for lost time.

"Look at him come!"

Both passengers stopped chopping ice to watch. Twenty miles of Bennett were behind them—room and to spare for the sea to toss up its mountains toward the sky. Sinking and soaring like a storm-god, the sailor drove by them. The huge sail seemed to grip the boat from the crests of the waves, to tear it bodily out of the water, and fling it crashing and smothering down into the yawning troughs.

"The sea'll never catch him!"

"But he'll r-r-run her nose under!"

Even as they spoke, the black tarpaulin swooped from sight behind a big comber. The next wave rolled over the spot, and the next, but the boat did not reappear. The *Alma* rushed by the place. A little riffraff of oats and boxes was seen. An arm thrust up and a shaggy head broke surface a score of yards away.

For a time there was silence. As the end of the lake came in sight, the waves began to leap aboard with such steady recurrence that the correspondents no longer chopped ice but flung the water out with buckets. Even this would not do, and, after a shouted conference with Rasmunsen, they attacked the baggage. Flour, bacon, beans, blankets, cooking-stove, ropes, odds and ends, everything they could get hands on, flew overboard. The boat acknowledged it at once, taking less water and rising more buoyantly.

"That'll do!" Rasmunsen called sternly, as they applied themselves to the top layer of eggs.

"The h-hell it will!" answered the shivering one, savagely. With the exception of their notes, films, and cameras, they had sacrificed their outfit. He bent over, laid hold of an egg-box, and began to worry it out from under the lashing.

"Drop it! Drop it, I say!"

Rasmunsen had managed to draw his revolver, and with the crook of his arm over the sweep head, was taking aim. The correspondent stood up on the thwart, balancing back and forth, his face twisted with menace and speechless anger.

"My God!"

So cried his brother correspondent, hurling himself, face downward, into the bottom of the boat. The *Alma*, under the divided attention of Rasmunsen, had been caught by a great mass of water and whirled around. The after leach hollowed, the sail emptied and jibed, and the boom, sweeping with terrific force across the boat, carried the angry correspondent overboard with a broken back. Mast and sail had gone over the side as well. A drenching sea followed, as the boat lost headway, and Rasmunsen sprang to the bailing bucket.

Several boats hurtled past them in the next half-hour,—small boats, boats of their own size, boats afraid, unable to do aught but run madly on. Then a ten-ton barge, at imminent risk of destruction, lowered sail to windward and lumbered down upon them.

"Keep off! Keep off!" Rasmunsen screamed.

But his low gunwale ground against the heavy craft, and the remaining correspondent clambered aboard. Rasmunsen was over the eggs like a cat and in the bow of the *Alma*, striving with numb fingers to bend the hauling-lines together.

"Come on!" a red-whiskered man yelled at him.

"I've a thousand dozen eggs here," he shouted back. "Gimme a tow! I'll pay you!"

"Come on!" they howled in chorus.

A big whitecap broke just beyond, washing over the barge and leaving the *Alma* half swamped. The men cast off, cursing him as they ran up their sail. Rasmunsen cursed back and fell to bailing. The mast and sail, like a sea anchor, still fast by the halyards, held the boat head on to wind and sea and gave him a chance to fight the water out.

Three hours later, numbed, exhausted, blathering like a lunatic, but still bailing, he went ashore on an ice-strewn beach near Cariboo Crossing. Two men, a government courier and a half-breed voyageur, dragged him out of the surf, saved his cargo, and beached the *Alma*. They were paddling out of the country in a Peterborough, and gave him shelter for the night in their storm-bound camp. Next morning they departed, but he elected to stay by his eggs. And thereafter the name and fame of the man with the thousand dozen eggs began to spread through the land. Gold-seekers who made in before the freeze-up carried the news of his coming. Grizzled old-timers of Forty Mile and Circle City, sour doughs with leathern jaws and bean-calloused stomachs, called up dream memories of chickens and green things at mention of his name. Dyea and Skaguay took an interest in his being, and questioned his progress from every man who came over the passes, while Dawson—golden, omeletless Dawson—fretted and worried, and way-laid every chance arrival for word of him.

But of this Rasmunsen knew nothing. The day after the wreck he patched up the *Alma* and pulled out. A cruel east wind blew in his teeth from Tagish, but he got the oars over the side and bucked manfully into it, though half the time he was drifting backward and chopping ice from the blades. According to the custom of the country, he was driven ashore at Windy Arm; three times on Tagish saw him swamped and beached; and Lake Marsh held him at the freeze-up. The *Alma* was crushed in the jamming of the floes, but the eggs were intact. These he back-tripped two miles across the ice to the shore, where he built a caché, which stood for years after and was pointed out by men who knew.

Half a thousand frozen miles stretched between him and Dawson, and the waterway was closed. But Rasmunsen, with a peculiar tense look in his face, struck back up the lakes on foot. What he suffered on that lone trip, with nought but a single blanket, an axe, and a handful of beans, is not given to ordinary mortals to know. Only the Arctic adventurer may understand. Suffice that he was caught in a blizzard on Chilkoot and left two of his toes with the surgeon at Sheep Camp. Yet he stood on his feet and washed dishes in the scullery of the *Pawona* to the Puget Sound, and from there passed coal on a P. S. boat to San Francisco.

It was a haggard, unkempt man who limped across the shining office floor to raise a second mortgage from the bank people. His hollow cheeks betrayed themselves through the scraggy beard, and his eyes seemed to have retired into deep caverns where they burned with cold fires. His hands were grained from exposure and hard work, and the nails were rimmed with tight-packed dirt and coal-dust. He spoke vaguely of eggs and ice-packs, winds and tides; but when they declined to let him have more than a second thousand, his talk became incoherent, concerning itself chiefly with the price of dogs and dog-food, and such things as snowshoes and moccasins and winter trails. They let him have fifteen hundred, which was more than the cottage warranted, and breathed easier when he scrawled his signature and passed out the door.

Two weeks later he went over Chilkoot with three dog sleds of five dogs each. One team he drove, the two Indians with him driving the others. At Lake Marsh they broke out the caché and loaded up. But there was no trail. He was the first in over the ice, and to him fell the task of packing the snow and hammering away through the rough river jams. Behind him he often observed a campfire smoke trickling thinly up through the quiet air, and he wondered why the people did not overtake him. For he was a stranger to the land and did not understand. Nor could he understand his Indians when they tried to explain. This they conceived to be a hardship, but when they balked and refused to break camp of mornings, he drove them to their work at pistol point.

When he slipped through an ice bridge near the White Horse and froze his foot, tender yet and oversensitive from the previous freezing, the Indians looked for him to lie up. But he sacrificed a blanket, and, with his foot incased in an enormous moccasin, big as a water-bucket, continued to take his regular turn with the front sled. Here was the cruellest work, and they respected him, though on the side they rapped their foreheads with their knuckles and significantly shook their heads. One night they tried to run away, but the zip-zip of his bullets in the snow brought them back, snarling but convinced. Whereupon, being only savage Chilkat men, they put their heads together to kill him; but he slept like a cat, and, waking or sleeping, the chance never came. Often they tried to tell him the import of the smoke wreath in the rear, but he could not comprehend and grew suspicious of them. And when they sulked or shirked, he was quick to let drive at them between the eyes, and quick to cool their heated souls with sight of his ready revolver.

And so it went—with mutinous men, wild dogs, and a trail that broke the heart. He fought the men to stay with him, fought the dogs to keep them away from the eggs, fought the ice, the cold, and the pain of his foot, which would not heal. As fast as the young tissue renewed, it was bitten and scared by the frost, so that a running sore developed, into which he could almost shove his fist. In the mornings, when he first put his weight upon it, his head went dizzy, and he was near to fainting from the pain; but later on in the day it usually grew numb, to recommence when he crawled into his blankets and tried to sleep. Yet he, who had been a clerk and sat at a desk all his days, toiled till the Indians were exhausted, and even out-worked the dogs. How hard he worked, how much he suffered, he did not know. Being a man of the one idea, now that the idea had come, it mastered him. In the foreground of his consciousness was Dawson, in the background his thousand dozen eggs, and midway between the two his ego fluttered, striving always to draw them together to a glittering golden point. This golden point was the five thousand dollars, the consummation of the idea and the point of departure for whatever new idea might present itself. For the rest, he was a mere automaton. He was unaware of other things, seeing them as through a glass darkly, and giving them no thought. The work of his hands he did with machine-like wisdom; likewise the work of his head. So the look on his face grew very tense, till even the Indians were afraid of it, and marvelled at the strange white man who had made them slaves and forced them to toil with such foolishness.

Then came a snap on Lake Le Barge, when the cold of outer space smote the tip of the planet, and the force ranged sixty and odd degrees below zero. Here, labouring with open mouth that he might breathe more freely, he chilled his lungs, and for the rest of the trip he was troubled with a dry, hacking cough, especially irritable in smoke of camp or under stress of undue exertion. On the Thirty Mile river he found much open water, spanned by precarious ice bridges and fringed with narrow rim ice, tricky and uncertain. The rim ice was impossible to reckon on, and he dared it without reckoning, falling back on his revolver when his drivers demurred. But on the ice bridges, covered with snow though they were, precautions could be taken. These they crossed on their snowshoes, with long poles, held crosswise in their hands, to which to cling in case of accident. Once over, the dogs were called to follow. And on such a bridge, where the absence of the centre ice was masked by the snow, one of the Indians met his end. He went through as quickly and neatly as a knife through thin cream, and the current swept him from view down under the stream ice.

That night his mate fled away through the pale moonlight, Rasmunsen futilely puncturing the silence with his revolver—a thing that he handled with more celerity than cleverness. Thirty-six hours later the Indian made a police camp on the Big Salmon.

"Um—um—um funny mans—what you call?—top um head all loose," the interpreter explained to the puzzled captain. "Eh? Yep, clazy, much clazy mans. Eggs, eggs, all a time eggs—savvy? Come bime-by."

It was several days before Rasmunsen arrived, the three sleds lashed together, and all the dogs in a single team. It was awkward, and where the going was bad he was compelled to back-trip it sled by sled, though he managed most of the time, through herculean efforts, to bring all along on the one haul. He did not seem moved when the captain of police told him his man was hitting the high places for Dawson, and was by that time, probably, half-way between Selkirk and Stewart. Nor did he appear interested when informed that the police had broken the trail as far as Pelly; for he had attained to a fatalistic acceptance of all natural dispensations, good or ill. But when they told him that Dawson was in the bitter clutch of famine, he smiled, threw the harness on his dogs, and pulled out.

But it was at his next halt that the mystery of the smoke was explained. With the word at Big Salmon that the trail was broken to Pelly, there was no longer any need for the smoke wreath to linger in his wake; and Rasmunsen, crouching over lonely fire, saw a motley string of sleds go by. First came the courier and the half-breed who had hauled him out from Bennett; then mail-carriers for Circle City, two sleds of them, and a mixed following of ingoing Klondikers. Dogs and men were fresh and fat, while Rasmunsen and his brutes were jaded and worn down to the skin and bone. They of the smoke wreath had travelled one day in three, resting and reserving their strength for the dash to come when broken trail was met with; while each day he had plunged and floundered forward, breaking the spirit of his dogs and robbing them of their mettle.

As for himself, he was unbreakable. They thanked him kindly for his efforts in their behalf, those fat, fresh men,—thanked him kindly, with broad grins and ribald laughter; and now, when he understood, he made no answer. Nor did he cherish silent bitterness. It was immaterial. The idea—the fact behind the idea—was not changed. Here he was and his thousand dozen; there was Dawson; the problem was unaltered.

At the Little Salmon, being short of dog food, the dogs got into his grub, and from there to Selkirk he lived on beans—coarse, brown beans, big beans, grossly nutritive, which griped his stomach and doubled him up at two-hour intervals. But the Factor at Selkirk had a notice on the door of the Post to the effect that no steamer had been up the Yukon for two years, and in consequence grub was beyond price. He offered to swap flour, however, at the rate of a cupful of each egg, but Rasmunsen shook his head and hit the trail. Below the Post he managed to buy frozen horse hide for the dogs, the horses having been slain by the Chilkat cattle men, and the scraps and offal preserved by the Indians. He tackled the hide himself, but the hair worked into the bean sores of his mouth, and was beyond endurance.

Here at Selkirk he met the forerunners of the hungry exodus of Dawson, and from there on they crept over the trail, a dismal throng. "No grub!" was the song they sang. "No grub, and had to go." "Everybody holding candles for a rise in the spring." "Flour dollar 'n a half a pound, and no sellers."

"Eggs?" one of them answered. "Dollar apiece, but there ain't none."

Rasmunsen made a rapid calculation. "Twelve thousand dollars," he said aloud.

"Hey?" the man asked.

"Nothing," he answered, and *mushed* the dogs along.

When he arrived at Stewart River, seventy from Dawson, five of his dogs were gone, and the remainder were falling in the traces. He, also, was in the traces, hauling with what little strength was left in him. Even then he was barely crawling along ten miles a day. His cheek-bones and nose, frost-bitten again and again, were turned bloody-black and hideous. The thumb, which was separated from the fingers by the gee-pole, had likewise been nipped and gave him great pain. The monstrous moccasin still incased his foot, and strange pains were beginning to rack the leg. At Sixty Mile, the last beans, which he had been rationing for some time, were finished; yet he steadfastly refused to touch the eggs. He could not reconcile his mind to the legitimacy of it, and staggered and fell along the way to Indian River. Here a fresh-killed moose and an open-handed old-timer gave him and his dogs new strength, and at Ainslie's he felt repaid for it all when a stampede, ripe from Dawson in five hours, was sure he could get a dollar and a quarter for every egg he possessed.

He came up the steep bank by the Dawson barracks with fluttering heart and shaking knees. The dogs were so weak that he was forced to rest them, and, waiting, he leaned limply against the gee-pole. A man, an eminently decorous-looking man, came sauntering by in a great bearskin coat. He glanced at Rasmunsen curiously, then stopped and ran a speculative eye over the dogs and the three lashed sleds.

"What you got?" he asked.

"Eggs," Rasmunsen answered huskily, hardly able to pitch his voice above a whisper.

"Eggs! Whoopee! Whoopee!" He sprang up into the air, gyrated madly, and finished with half-a-dozen war steps. "You don't say—all of 'em?"

"All of 'em."

"Say, you must be the Egg Man." He walked around and viewed Rasmunsen from the other side. "Come, now, ain't you the Egg Man?"

Rasmunsen didn't know, but supposed he was, and the man sobered down a bit.

"What d'ye expect to get for 'em?" he asked cautiously.

Rasmunsen became audacious. "Dollar 'n a half," he said.

"Done!" the man came back promptly. "Gimme a dozen."

"I—I mean a dollar 'n a half apiece," Rasmunsen hesitatingly explained.

"Sure. I heard you. Make it two dozen. Here's the dust."

The man pulled out a healthy gold sack the size of a small sausage and knocked it negligently against the gee-pole. Rasmunsen felt a strange trembling in the pit of his stomach, a tickling of the nostrils, and an almost overwhelming desire to sit down and cry. But a curious, wide-eyed crowd was beginning to collect, and man after man was calling out for eggs. He was without scales, but the man with the bearskin coat fetched a pair and obligingly weighed in the dust while Rasmunsen passed out the goods. Soon there was a pushing and shoving and shouldering, and a great clamour. Everybody wanted to buy and to be served first. And as the excitement grew, Rasmunsen cooled down. This would never do. There must be something behind the fact of their buying so eagerly. It would be wiser if he rested first and sized up the market. Perhaps eggs were worth two dollars apiece. Anyway, whenever he wished to sell, he was sure of a dollar and a half. "Stop!" he cried, when a couple of hundred had been sold. "No more now. I'm played out. I've got to get a cabin, and then you can come and see me."

A groan went up at this, but the man with the bearskin coat approved. Twenty-four of the frozen eggs went rattling in his capacious pockets, and he didn't care whether the rest of the town ate or not. Besides, he could see Rasmunsen was on his last legs.

"There's a cabin right around the second corner from the Monte Carlo," he told him—"the one with the sody-bottle window. It ain't mine, but I've got charge of it. Rents for ten a day and cheap for the money. You move right in, and I'll see you later. Don't forget the sody-bottle window."

"Tra-la-loo!" he called back a moment later. "I'm goin' up the hill to eat eggs and dream of home."

On his way to the cabin, Rasmunsen recollected he was hungry and bought a small supply of provisions at the N. A. T. & T. store—also a beefsteak at the butcher shop and dried salmon for the dogs. He found the cabin without difficulty, and left the dogs in the harness while he started the fire and got the coffee under way.

"A dollar 'n a half apiece—one thousand dozen—eighteen thousand dollars!" he kept muttering it to himself, over and over, as he went about his work.

As he flopped the steak into the frying-pan the door opened. He turned. It was the man with the bearskin coat. He seemed to come in with determination, as though bound on some explicit errand, but as he looked at Rasmunsen an expression of perplexity came into his face.

"I say—now I say—" he began, then halted.

Rasmunsen wondered if he wanted the rent.

"I say, damn it, you know, them eggs is bad."

Rasmunsen staggered. He felt as though some one had struck him an astounding blow between the eyes. The walls of the cabin reeled and tilted up. He put out his hand to steady himself and rested it on the stove. The sharp pain and the smell of the burning flesh brought him back to himself.

"I see," he said slowly, fumbling in his pocket for the sack. "You want your money back."

"It ain't the money," the man said, "but hain't you got any eggs—good?"

Rasmunsen shook his head. "You'd better take the money."

But the man refused and backed away. "I'll come back," he said, "when you've taken stock, and get what's comin'."

Rasmunsen rolled the chopping-block into the cabin and carried in the eggs. He went about it quite calmly. He took up the hand-axe, and, one by one, chopped the eggs in half. These halves he examined carefully and let fall to the floor. At first he sampled from the different cases, then deliberately emptied one case at a time. The heap on the floor grew larger. The coffee boiled over and the smoke of the burning beefsteak filled the cabin. He chopped steadfastly and monotonously till the last case was finished.

Somebody knocked at the door, knocked again, and let himself in.

"What a mess!" he remarked, as he paused and surveyed the scene.

The severed eggs were beginning to thaw in the heat of the stove, and a miserable odor was growing stronger.

"Must a-happened on the steamer," he suggested.

Rasmunsen looked at him long and blankly.

"I'm Murray, Big Jim Murray, everybody knows me," the man volunteered. "I'm just hearin' your eggs is rotten, and I'm offerin' you two hundred for the batch. They ain't good as salmon, but still they're fair scoffin's for dogs."

Rasmunsen seemed turned to stone. He did not move. "You go to hell," he said passionlessly.

"Now just consider. I pride myself it's a decent price for a mess like that, and it's better 'n nothin'. Two hundred. What you say?"

"You go to hell," Rasmunsen repeated softly, "and get out of here."

Murray gaped with a great awe, then went out carefully, backward, with his eyes fixed an the other's face.

Rasmunsen followed him out and turned the dogs loose. He threw them all the salmon he had bought, and coiled a sled-lashing up in his hand. Then he re-entered the cabin and drew the latch in after him. The smoke from the cindered steak made his eyes smart. He stood on the bunk, passed the lashing over the ridge-pole, and measured the swing-off with his eye. It did not seem to satisfy, for he put the stool on the bunk and climbed upon the stool. He drove a noose in the end of the lashing and slipped his head through. The other end he made fast. Then he kicked the stool out from under.

# LOVE OF LIFE

"This out of all will remain—
    They have lived and have tossed:
So much of the game will be gain,
    Though the gold of the dice has been lost."

THEY limped painfully down the bank, and once the foremost of the two men staggered among the rough-strewn rocks. They were tired and weak, and their faces had the drawn expression of patience which comes of hardship long endured. They were heavily burdened with blanket packs which were strapped to their shoulders. Head-straps, passing across the forehead, helped support these packs. Each man carried a rifle. They walked in a stooped posture, the shoulders well forward, the head still farther forward, the eyes bent upon the ground.

"I wish we had just about two of them cartridges that's layin' in that cache of ourn," said the second man.

His voice was utterly and drearily expressionless. He spoke without enthusiasm; and the first man, limping into the milky stream that foamed over the rocks, vouchsafed no reply.

The other man followed at his heels. They did not remove their foot-gear, though the water was icy cold—so cold that their ankles ached and their feet went numb. In places the water dashed against their knees, and both men staggered for footing.

The man who followed slipped on a smooth boulder, nearly fell, but recovered himself with a violent effort, at the same time uttering a sharp exclamation of pain. He seemed faint and dizzy and put out his free hand while he reeled, as though seeking support against the air. When he had steadied himself he stepped forward, but reeled again and nearly fell. Then he stood still and looked at the other man, who had never turned his head.

The man stood still for fully a minute, as though debating with himself. Then he called out:

"I say, Bill, I've sprained my ankle."

Bill staggered on through the milky water. He did not look around. The man watched him go, and though his face was expressionless as ever, his eyes were like the eyes of a wounded deer.

The other man limped up the farther bank and continued straight on without looking back. The man in the stream watched him. His lips trembled a little, so that the rough thatch of brown hair which covered them was visibly agitated. His tongue even strayed out to moisten them.

"Bill!" he cried out.

It was the pleading cry of a strong man in distress, but Bill's head did not turn. The man watched him go, limping grotesquely and lurching forward with stammering gait up the slow slope toward the soft sky-line of the low-lying hill. He watched him go till he passed over the crest and disappeared. Then he turned his gaze and slowly took in the circle of the world that remained to him now that Bill was gone.

Near the horizon the sun was smouldering dimly, almost obscured by formless mists and vapors, which gave an impression of mass and density without outline or tangibility. The man pulled out his watch, the while resting his weight on one leg. It was four o'clock, and as the season was near the last of July or first of August,—he did not know the precise date within a week or two,—he knew that the sun roughly marked the northwest. He looked to the south and knew that somewhere beyond those bleak hills lay the Great Bear Lake; also, he knew that in that direction the Arctic Circle cut its forbidding way across the Canadian Barrens. This stream in which he stood was a feeder to the Coppermine River, which in turn flowed north and emptied into Coronation Gulf and the Arctic Ocean. He had never been there, but he had seen it, once, on a Hudson Bay Company chart.

Again his gaze completed the circle of the world about him. It was not a heartening spectacle. Everywhere was soft sky-line. The hills were all low-lying. There were no trees, no shrubs, no grasses—naught but a tremendous and terrible desolation that sent fear swiftly dawning into his eyes.

"Bill!" he whispered, once and twice; "Bill!"

He cowered in the midst of the milky water, as though the vastness were pressing in upon him with overwhelming force, brutally crushing him with its complacent awfulness. He began to shake as with an ague-fit, till the gun fell from his hand with a splash. This served to rouse him. He fought with his fear and pulled himself together, groping in the water and recovering the weapon. He hitched his pack farther over on his left shoulder, so as to take a portion of its weight from off the injured ankle. Then he proceeded, slowly and carefully, wincing with pain, to the bank.

He did not stop. With a desperation that was madness, unmindful of the pain, he hurried up the slope to the crest of the hill over which his comrade had disappeared—more grotesque and comical by far than that limping, jerking comrade. But at the crest he saw a shallow valley, empty of life. He fought with his fear again, overcame it, hitched the pack still farther over on his left shoulder, and lurched on down the slope.

The bottom of the valley was soggy with water, which the thick moss held, spongelike, close to the surface. This water squirted out from under his feet at every step, and each time he lifted a foot the action culminated in a sucking sound as the wet moss reluctantly released its grip. He picked his way from muskeg to muskeg, and followed the other man's footsteps along and across the rocky ledges which thrust like islets through the sea of moss.

Though alone, he was not lost. Farther on he knew he would come to where dead spruce and fir, very small and weazened, bordered the shore of a little lake, the *titchinnichilie*, in the tongue of the country, the "land of little sticks." And into that lake flowed a small stream, the water of which was not milky. There was rush-grass on that stream—this he remembered well—but no timber, and he would follow it till its first trickle ceased at a divide. He would cross this divide to the first trickle of another stream, flowing to the west, which he would follow until it emptied into the river Dease, and here he would find a cache under an upturned canoe and piled over with many rocks. And in this cache would be ammunition for his empty gun, fish-hooks and lines, a small net—all the utilities for the killing and snaring of food. Also, he would find flour,—not much,—a piece of bacon, and some beans.

Bill would be waiting for him there, and they would paddle away south down the Dease to the Great Bear Lake. And south across the lake they would go, ever south, till they gained the Mackenzie. And south, still south, they would go, while the winter raced vainly after them, and the ice formed in the eddies, and the days grew chill and crisp, south to some warm Hudson Bay Company post, where timber grew tall and generous and there was grub without end.

These were the thoughts of the man as he strove onward. But hard as he strove with his body, he strove equally hard with his mind, trying to think that Bill had not deserted him, that Bill would surely wait for him at the cache. He was compelled to think this thought, or else there would not be any use to strive, and he would have lain down and died. And as the dim ball of the sun sank slowly into the northwest he covered every inch—and many times—of his and Bill's flight south before the downcoming winter. And he conned the grub of the cache and the grub of the Hudson Bay Company post over and over again. He had not eaten for two days; for a far longer time he had not had all he wanted to eat. Often he stooped and picked pale muskeg berries, put them into his mouth, and chewed and swallowed them. A muskeg berry is a bit of seed enclosed in a bit of water. In the mouth the water melts away and the seed chews sharp and bitter. The man knew there was no nourishment in the berries, but he chewed them patiently with a hope greater than knowledge and defying experience.

At nine o'clock he stubbed his toe on a rocky ledge, and from sheer weariness and weakness staggered and fell. He lay for some time, without movement, on his side. Then he slipped out of the pack-straps and clumsily dragged himself into a sitting posture. It was not yet dark, and in the lingering twilight he groped about among the rocks for shreds of dry moss. When he had gathered a heap he built a fire,—a smouldering, smudgy fire,—and put a tin pot of water on to boil.

He unwrapped his pack and the first thing he did was to count his matches. There were sixty-seven. He counted them three times to make sure. He divided them into several portions, wrapping them in oil paper, disposing of one bunch in his empty tobacco pouch, of another bunch in the inside band of his battered hat, of a third bunch under his shirt on the chest. This accomplished, a panic came upon him, and he unwrapped them all and counted them again. There were still sixty-seven.

He dried his wet foot-gear by the fire. The moccasins were in soggy shreds. The blanket socks were worn through in places, and his feet were raw and bleeding. His ankle was throbbing, and he gave it an examination. It had swollen to the size of his knee. He tore a long strip from one of his two blankets and bound the ankle tightly. He tore other strips and bound them about his feet to serve for both moccasins and socks. Then he drank the pot of water, steaming hot, wound his watch, and crawled between his blankets.

He slept like a dead man. The brief darkness around midnight came and went. The sun arose in the north-east—at least the day dawned in that quarter, for the sun was hidden by gray clouds.

At six o'clock he awoke, quietly lying on his back. He gazed straight up into the gray sky and knew that he was hungry. As he rolled over on his elbow he was startled by a loud snort, and saw a bull caribou regarding him with alert curiosity. The animal was not mere than fifty feet away, and instantly into the man's mind leaped the vision and the savor of a caribou steak sizzling and frying over a fire. Mechanically he reached for the empty gun, drew a bead, and pulled the trigger. The bull snorted and leaped away, his hoofs rattling and clattering as he fled across the ledges.

The man cursed and flung the empty gun from him. He groaned aloud as he started to drag himself to his feet. It was a slow and arduous task.

His joints were like rusty hinges. They worked harshly in their sockets, with much friction, and each bending or unbending was accomplished only through a sheer exertion of will. When he finally gained his feet, another minute or so was consumed in straightening up, so that he could stand erect as a man should stand.

He crawled up a small knoll and surveyed the prospect. There were no trees, no bushes, nothing but a gray sea of moss scarcely diversified by gray rocks, gray lakelets, and gray streamlets. The sky was gray. There was no sun nor hint of sun. He had no idea of north, and he had forgotten the way he had come to this spot the night before. But he was not lost. He knew that. Soon he would come to the land of the little sticks. He felt that it lay off to the left somewhere, not far—possibly just over the next low hill.

He went back to put his pack into shape for travelling. He assured himself of the existence of his three separate parcels of matches, though he did not stop to count them. But he did linger, debating, over a squat moose-hide sack. It was not large. He could hide it under his two hands. He knew that it weighed fifteen pounds,—as much as all the rest of the pack,—and it worried him. He finally set it to one side and proceeded to roll the pack. He paused to gaze at the squat moose-hide sack. He picked it up hastily with a defiant glance about him, as though the desolation were trying to rob him of it; and when he rose to his feet to stagger on into the day, it was included in the pack on his back.

He bore away to the left, stopping now and again to eat muskeg berries. His ankle had stiffened, his limp was more pronounced, but the pain of it was as nothing compared with the pain of his stomach. The hunger pangs were sharp. They gnawed and gnawed until he could not keep his mind steady on the course he must pursue to gain the land of little sticks. The muskeg berries did not allay this gnawing, while they made his tongue and the roof of his mouth sore with their irritating bite.

He came upon a valley where rock ptarmigan rose on whirring wings from the ledges and muskegs. Ker—ker—ker was the cry they made. He threw stones at them, but could not hit them. He placed his pack on the ground and stalked them as a cat stalks a sparrow. The sharp rocks cut through his pants' legs till his knees left a trail of blood; but the hurt was lost in the hurt of his hunger. He squirmed over the wet moss, saturating his clothes and chilling his body; but he was not aware of it, so great was his fever for food. And always the ptarmigan rose, whirring, before him, till their ker—ker—ker became a mock to him, and he cursed them and cried aloud at them with their own cry.

Once he crawled upon one that must have been asleep. He did not see it till it shot up in his face from its rocky nook. He made a clutch as startled as was the rise of the ptarmigan, and there remained in his hand three tail-feathers. As he watched its flight he hated it, as though it had done him some terrible wrong. Then he returned and shouldered his pack.

As the day wore along he came into valleys or swales where game was more plentiful. A band of caribou passed by, twenty and odd animals, tantalizingly within rifle range. He felt a wild desire to run after them, a certitude that he could run them down. A black fox came toward him, carrying a ptarmigan in his mouth. The man shouted. It was a fearful cry, but the fox, leaping away in fright, did not drop the ptarmigan.

Late in the afternoon he followed a stream, milky with lime, which ran through sparse patches of rush-grass. Grasping these rushes firmly near the root, he pulled up what resembled a young onion-sprout no larger than a shingle-nail. It was tender, and his teeth sank into it with a crunch that promised deliciously of food. But its fibers were tough. It was composed of stringy filaments saturated with water, like the berries, and devoid of nourishment. He threw off his pack and went into the rush-grass on hands and knees, crunching and munching, like some bovine creature.

He was very weary and often wished to rest—to lie down and sleep; but he was continually driven on—not so much by his desire to gain the land of little sticks as by his hunger. He searched little ponds for frogs and dug up the earth with his nails for worms, though he knew in spite that neither frogs nor worms existed so far north.

He looked into every pool of water vainly, until, as the long twilight came on, he discovered a solitary fish, the size of a minnow, in such a pool. He plunged his arm in up to the shoulder, but it eluded him. He reached for it with both hands and stirred up the milky mud at the bottom. In his excitement he fell in, wetting himself to the waist. Then the water was too muddy to admit of his seeing the fish, and he was compelled to wait until the sediment had settled.

The pursuit was renewed, till the water was again muddied. But he could not wait. He unstrapped the tin bucket and began to bale the pool. He baled wildly at first, splashing himself and flinging the water so short a distance that it ran back into the pool. He worked more carefully, striving to be cool, though his heart was pounding against his chest and his hands were trembling. At the end of half an hour the pool was nearly dry. Not a cupful of water remained. And there was no fish. He found a hidden crevice among the stones through which it had escaped to the adjoining and larger pool—a pool which he could not empty in a night and a day. Had he known of the crevice, he could have closed it with a rock at the beginning and the fish would have been his.

Thus he thought, and crumpled up and sank down upon the wet earth. At first he cried softly to himself, then he cried loudly to the pitiless desolation that ringed him around; and for a long time after he was shaken by great dry sobs.

He built a fire and warmed himself by drinking quarts of hot water, and made camp on a rocky ledge in the same fashion he had the night before. The last thing he did was to see that his matches were dry and to wind his watch. The blankets were wet and clammy. His ankle pulsed with pain. But he knew only that he was hungry, and through his restless sleep he dreamed of feasts and banquets and of food served and spread in all imaginable ways.

He awoke chilled and sick. There was no sun. The gray of earth and sky had become deeper, more profound. A raw wind was blowing, and the first flurries of snow were whitening the hilltops. The air about him thickened and grew white while he made a fire and boiled more water. It was wet snow, half rain, and the flakes were large and soggy. At first they melted as soon as they came in contact with the earth, but ever more fell, covering the ground, putting out the fire, spoiling his supply of moss-fuel.

This was a signal for him to strap on his pack and stumble onward, he knew not where. He was not concerned with the land of little sticks, nor with Bill and the cache under the upturned canoe by the river Dease. He was mastered by the verb "to eat." He was hunger-mad. He took no heed of the course he pursued, so long as that course led him through the swale bottoms. He felt his way through the wet snow to the watery muskeg berries, and went by feel as he pulled up the rush-grass by the roots. But it was tasteless stuff and did not satisfy. He found a weed that tasted sour and he ate all he could find of it, which was not much, for it was a creeping growth, easily hidden under the several inches of snow.

He had no fire that night, nor hot water, and crawled under his blanket to sleep the broken hunger-sleep. The snow turned into a cold rain. He awakened many times to feel it falling on his upturned face. Day came—a gray day and no sun. It had ceased raining. The keenness of his hunger had departed. Sensibility, as far as concerned the yearning for food, had been exhausted. There was a dull, heavy ache in his stomach, but it did not bother him so much. He was more rational, and once more he was chiefly interested in the land of little sticks and the cache by the river Dease.

He ripped the remnant of one of his blankets into strips and bound his bleeding feet. Also, he recinched the injured ankle and prepared himself for a day of travel. When he came to his pack, he paused long over the squat moose-hide sack, but in the end it went with him.

The snow had melted under the rain, and only the hilltops showed white. The sun came out, and he succeeded in locating the points of the compass, though he knew now that he was lost. Perhaps, in his previous days' wanderings, he had edged away too far to the left. He now bore off to the right to counteract the possible deviation from his true course.

Though the hunger pangs were no longer so exquisite, he realized that he was weak. He was compelled to pause for frequent rests, when he attacked the muskeg berries and rush-grass patches. His tongue felt dry and large, as though covered with a fine hairy growth, and it tasted bitter in his mouth. His heart gave him a great deal of trouble. When he had travelled a few minutes it would begin a remorseless thump, thump, thump, and then leap up and away in a painful flutter of beats that choked him and made him go faint and dizzy.

In the middle of the day he found two minnows in a large pool. It was impossible to bale it, but he was calmer now and managed to catch them in his tin bucket. They were no longer than his little finger, but he was not particularly hungry. The dull ache in his stomach had been growing duller and fainter. It seemed almost that his stomach was dozing. He ate the fish raw, masticating with painstaking care, for the eating was an act of pure reason. While he had no desire to eat, he knew that he must eat to live.

In the evening he caught three more minnows, eating two and saving the third for breakfast. The sun had dried stray shreds of moss, and he was able to warm himself with hot water. He had not covered more than ten miles that day; and the next day, travelling whenever his heart permitted him, he covered no more than five miles. But his stomach did not give him the slightest uneasiness. It had gone to sleep. He was in a strange country, too, and the caribou were growing more plentiful, also the wolves. Often their yelps drifted across the desolation, and once he saw three of them slinking away before his path.

Another night; and in the morning, being more rational, he untied the leather string that fastened the squat moose-hide sack. From its open mouth poured a yellow stream of coarse gold-dust and nuggets. He roughly divided the gold in halves, caching one half on a prominent ledge, wrapped in a piece of blanket, and returning the other half to the sack. He also began to use strips of the one remaining blanket for his feet. He still clung to his gun, for there were cartridges in that cache by the river Dease.

This was a day of fog, and this day hunger awoke in him again. He was very weak and was afflicted with a giddiness which at times blinded him. It was no uncommon thing now for him to stumble and fall; and stumbling once, he fell squarely into a ptarmigan nest. There were four newly hatched chicks, a day old—little specks of pulsating life no more than a mouthful; and he ate them ravenously, thrusting them alive into his mouth and crunching them like egg-shells between his teeth. The mother ptarmigan beat about him with great outcry. He used his gun as a club with which to knock her over, but she dodged out of reach. He threw stones at her and with one chance shot broke a wing. Then she fluttered away, running, trailing the broken wing, with him in pursuit.

The little chicks had no more than whetted his appetite. He hopped and bobbed clumsily along on his injured ankle, throwing stones and screaming hoarsely at times; at other times hopping and bobbing silently along, picking himself up grimly and patiently when he fell, or rubbing his eyes with his hand when the giddiness threatened to overpower him.

The chase led him across swampy ground in the bottom of the valley, and he came upon footprints in the soggy moss. They were not his own—he could see that. They must be Bill's. But he could not stop, for the mother ptarmigan was running on. He would catch her first, then he would return and investigate.

He exhausted the mother ptarmigan; but he exhausted himself. She lay panting on her side. He lay panting on his side, a dozen feet away, unable to crawl to her. And as he recovered she recovered, fluttering out of reach as his hungry hand went out to her. The chase was resumed. Night settled down and she escaped. He stumbled from weakness and pitched head foremost on his face, cutting his cheek, his pack upon his back. He did not move for a long while; then he rolled over on his side, wound his watch, and lay there until morning.

Another day of fog. Half of his last blanket had gone into foot-wrappings. He failed to pick up Bill's trail. It did not matter. His hunger was driving him too compellingly—only—only he wondered if Bill, too, were lost. By midday the irk of his pack became too oppressive. Again he divided the gold, this time merely spilling half of it on the ground. In the afternoon he threw the rest of it away, there remaining to him only the half-blanket, the tin bucket, and the rifle.

An hallucination began to trouble him. He felt confident that one cartridge remained to him. It was in the chamber of the rifle and he had overlooked it. On the other hand, he knew all the time that the chamber was empty. But the hallucination persisted. He fought it off for hours, then threw his rifle open and was confronted with emptiness. The disappointment was as bitter as though he had really expected to find the cartridge.

He plodded on for half an hour, when the hallucination arose again. Again he fought it, and still it persisted, till for very relief he opened his rifle to unconvince himself. At times his mind wandered farther afield, and he plodded on, a mere automaton, strange conceits and whimsicalities gnawing at his brain like worms. But these excursions out of the real were of brief duration, for ever the pangs of the hunger-bite called him back. He was jerked back abruptly once from such an excursion by a sight that caused him nearly to faint. He reeled and swayed, doddering like a drunken man to keep from falling. Before him stood a horse. A horse! He could not believe his eyes. A thick mist was in them, intershot with sparkling points of light. He rubbed his eyes savagely to clear his vision, and beheld, not a horse, but a great brown bear. The animal was studying him with bellicose curiosity.

The man had brought his gun halfway to his shoulder before he realized. He lowered it and drew his hunting-knife from its beaded sheath at his hip. Before him was meat and life. He ran his thumb along the edge of his knife. It was sharp. The point was sharp. He would fling himself upon the bear and kill it. But his heart began its warning thump, thump, thump. Then followed the wild upward leap and tattoo of flutters, the pressing as of an iron band about his forehead, the creeping of the dizziness into his brain.

His desperate courage was evicted by a great surge of fear. In his weakness, what if the animal attacked him? He drew himself up to his most imposing stature, gripping the knife and staring hard at the bear. The bear advanced clumsily a couple of steps, reared up, and gave vent to a tentative growl. If the man ran, he would run after him; but the man did not run. He was animated now with the courage of fear. He, too, growled, savagely, terribly, voicing the fear that is to life germane and that lies twisted about life's deepest roots.

The bear edged away to one side, growling menacingly, himself appalled by this mysterious creature that appeared upright and unafraid. But the man did not move. He stood like a statue till the danger was past, when he yielded to a fit of trembling and sank down into the wet moss.

He pulled himself together and went on, afraid now in a new way. It was not the fear that he should die passively from lack of food, but that he should be destroyed violently before starvation had exhausted the last particle of the endeavor in him that made toward surviving. There were the wolves. Back and forth across the desolation drifted their howls, weaving the very air into a fabric of menace that was so tangible that he found himself, arms in the air, pressing it back from him as it might be the walls of a wind-blown tent.

Now and again the wolves, in packs of two and three, crossed his path. But they sheered clear of him. They were not in sufficient numbers, and besides they were hunting the caribou, which did not battle, while this strange creature that walked erect might scratch and bite.

In the late afternoon he came upon scattered bones where the wolves had made a kill. The debris had been a caribou calf an hour before, squawking and running and very much alive. He contemplated the bones, clean-picked and polished, pink with the cell-life in them which had not yet died. Could it possibly be that he might be that ere the day was done! Such was life, eh? A vain and fleeting thing. It was only life that pained. There was no hurt in death. To die was to sleep. It meant cessation, rest. Then why was he not content to die?

But he did not moralize long. He was squatting in the moss, a bone in his mouth, sucking at the shreds of life that still dyed it faintly pink. The sweet meaty taste, thin and elusive almost as a memory, maddened him. He closed his jaws on the bones and crunched. Sometimes it was the bone that broke, sometimes his teeth. Then he crushed the bones between rocks, pounded them to a pulp, and swallowed them. He pounded his fingers, too, in his haste, and yet found a moment in which to feel surprise at the fact that his fingers did not hurt much when caught under the descending rock.

Came frightful days of snow and rain. He did not know when he made camp, when he broke camp. He travelled in the night as much as in the day. He rested wherever he fell, crawled on whenever the dying life in him flickered up and burned less dimly. He, as a man, no longer strove. It was the life in him, unwilling to die, that drove him on. He did not suffer. His nerves had become blunted, numb, while his mind was filled with weird visions and delicious dreams.

But ever he sucked and chewed on the crushed bones of the caribou calf, the least remnants of which he had gathered up and carried with him. He crossed no more hills or divides, but automatically followed a large stream which flowed through a wide and shallow valley. He did not see this stream nor this valley. He saw nothing save visions. Soul and body walked or crawled side by side, yet apart, so slender was the thread that bound them.

He awoke in his right mind, lying on his back on a rocky ledge. The sun was shining bright and warm. Afar off he heard the squawking of caribou calves. He was aware of vague memories of rain and wind and snow, but whether he had been beaten by the storm for two days or two weeks he did not know.

For some time he lay without movement, the genial sunshine pouring upon him and saturating his miserable body with its warmth. A fine day, he thought. Perhaps he could manage to locate himself. By a painful effort he rolled over on his side. Below him flowed a wide and sluggish river. Its unfamiliarity puzzled him. Slowly he followed it with his eyes, winding in wide sweeps among the bleak, bare hills, bleaker and barer and lower-lying than any hills he had yet encountered. Slowly, deliberately, without excitement or more than the most casual interest, he followed the course of the strange stream toward the sky-line and saw it emptying into a bright and shining sea. He was still unexcited. Most unusual, he thought, a vision or a mirage—more likely a vision, a trick of his disordered mind. He was confirmed in this by sight of a ship lying at anchor in the midst of the shining sea. He closed his eyes for a while, then opened them. Strange how the vision persisted! Yet not strange. He knew there were no seas or ships in the heart of the barren lands, just as he had known there was no cartridge in the empty rifle.

He heard a snuffle behind him—a half-choking gasp or cough. Very slowly, because of his exceeding weakness and stiffness, he rolled over on his other side. He could see nothing near at hand, but he waited patiently. Again came the snuffle and cough, and outlined between two jagged rocks not a score of feet away he made out the gray head of a wolf. The sharp ears were not pricked so sharply as he had seen them on other wolves; the eyes were bleared and bloodshot, the head seemed to droop limply and forlornly. The animal blinked continually in the sunshine. It seemed sick. As he looked it snuffled and coughed again.

This, at least, was real, he thought, and turned on the other side so that he might see the reality of the world which had been veiled from him before by the vision. But the sea still shone in the distance and the ship was plainly discernible. Was it reality, after all? He closed his eyes for a long while and thought, and then it came to him. He had been making north by east, away from the Dease Divide and into the Coppermine Valley. This wide and sluggish river was the Coppermine. That shining sea was the Arctic Ocean. That ship was a whaler, strayed east, far east, from the mouth of the Mackenzie, and it was lying at anchor in Coronation Gulf. He remembered the Hudson Bay Company chart he had seen long ago, and it was all clear and reasonable to him.

He sat up and turned his attention to immediate affairs. He had worn through the blanket-wrappings, and his feet were shapeless lumps of raw meat. His last blanket was gone. Rifle and knife were both missing. He had lost his hat somewhere, with the bunch of matches in the band, but the matches against his chest were safe and dry inside the tobacco pouch and oil paper. He looked at his watch. It marked eleven o'clock and was still running. Evidently he had kept it wound.

He was calm and collected. Though extremely weak, he had no sensation of pain. He was not hungry. The thought of food was not even pleasant to him, and whatever he did was done by his reason alone. He ripped off his pants' legs to the knees and bound them about his feet. Somehow he had succeeded in retaining the tin bucket. He would have some hot water before he began what he foresaw was to be a terrible journey to the ship.

His movements were slow. He shook as with a palsy. When he started to collect dry moss, he found he could not rise to his feet. He tried again and again, then contented himself with crawling about on hands and knees. Once he crawled near to the sick wolf. The animal dragged itself reluctantly out of his way, licking its chops with a tongue which seemed hardly to have the strength to curl. The man noticed that the tongue was not the customary healthy red. It was a yellowish brown and seemed coated with a rough and half-dry mucus.

After he had drunk a quart of hot water the man found he was able to stand, and even to walk as well as a dying man might be supposed to walk. Every minute or so he was compelled to rest. His steps were feeble and uncertain, just as the wolf's that trailed him were feeble and uncertain; and that night, when the shining sea was blotted out by blackness, he knew he was nearer to it by no more than four miles.

Throughout the night he heard the cough of the sick wolf, and now and then the squawking of the caribou calves. There was life all around him, but it was strong life, very much alive and well, and he knew the sick wolf clung to the sick man's trail in the hope that the man would die first. In the morning, on opening his eyes, he beheld it regarding him with a wistful and hungry stare. It stood crouched, with tail between its legs, like a miserable and woe-begone dog. It shivered in the chill morning wind, and grinned dispiritedly when the man spoke to it in a voice that achieved no more than a hoarse whisper.

The sun rose brightly, and all morning the man tottered and fell toward the ship on the shining sea. The weather was perfect. It was the brief Indian Summer of the high latitudes. It might last a week. To-morrow or next day it might be gone.

In the afternoon the man came upon a trail. It was of another man, who did not walk, but who dragged himself on all fours. The man thought it might be Bill, but he thought in a dull, uninterested way. He had no curiosity. In fact, sensation and emotion had left him. He was no longer susceptible to pain. Stomach and nerves had gone to sleep. Yet the life that was in him drove him on. He was very weary, but it refused to die. It was because it refused to die that he still ate muskeg berries and minnows, drank his hot water, and kept a wary eye on the sick wolf.

He followed the trail of the other man who dragged himself along, and soon came to the end of it—a few fresh-picked bones where the soggy moss was marked by the foot-pads of many wolves. He saw a squat moose-hide sack, mate to his own, which had been torn by sharp teeth. He picked it up, though its weight was almost too much for his feeble fingers. Bill had carried it to the last. Ha! ha! He would have the laugh on Bill. He would survive and carry it to the ship in the shining sea. His mirth was hoarse and ghastly, like a raven's croak, and the sick wolf joined him, howling lugubriously. The man ceased suddenly. How could he have the laugh on Bill if that were Bill; if those bones, so pinky-white and clean, were Bill?

He turned away. Well, Bill had deserted him; but he would not take the gold, nor would he suck Bill's bones. Bill would have, though, had it been the other way around, he mused as he staggered on.

He came to a pool of water. Stooping over in quest of minnows, he jerked his head back as though he had been stung. He had caught sight of his reflected face. So horrible was it that sensibility awoke long enough to be shocked. There were three minnows in the pool, which was too large to drain; and after several ineffectual attempts to catch them in the tin bucket he forbore. He was afraid, because of his great weakness, that he might fall in and drown. It was for this reason that he did not trust himself to the river astride one of the many drift-logs which lined its sand-spits.

That day he decreased the distance between him and the ship by three miles; the next day by two—for he was crawling now as Bill had crawled; and the end of the fifth day found the ship still seven miles away and him unable to make even a mile a day. Still the Indian Summer held on, and he continued to crawl and faint, turn and turn about; and ever the sick wolf coughed and wheezed at his heels. His knees had become raw meat like his feet, and though he padded them with the shirt from his back it was a red track he left behind him on the moss and stones. Once, glancing back, he saw the wolf licking hungrily his bleeding trail, and he saw sharply what his own end might be—unless—unless he could get the wolf. Then began as grim a tragedy of existence as was ever played—a sick man that crawled, a sick wolf that limped, two creatures dragging their dying carcasses across the desolation and hunting each other's lives.

Had it been a well wolf, it would not have mattered so much to the man; but the thought of going to feed the maw of that loathsome and all but dead thing was repugnant to him. He was finicky. His mind had begun to wander again, and to be perplexed by hallucinations, while his lucid intervals grew rarer and shorter.

He was awakened once from a faint by a wheeze close in his ear. The wolf leaped lamely back, losing its footing and falling in its weakness. It was ludicrous, but he was not amused. Nor was he even afraid. He was too far gone for that. But his mind was for the moment clear, and he lay and considered. The ship was no more than four miles away. He could see it quite distinctly when he rubbed the mists out of his eyes, and he could see the white sail of a small boat cutting the water of the shining sea. But he could never crawl those four miles. He knew that, and was very calm in the knowledge. He knew that he could not crawl half a mile. And yet he wanted to live. It was unreasonable that he should die after all he had undergone. Fate asked too much of him. And, dying, he declined to die. It was stark madness, perhaps, but in the very grip of Death he defied Death and refused to die.

He closed his eyes and composed himself with infinite precaution. He steeled himself to keep above the suffocating languor that lapped like a rising tide through all the wells of his being. It was very like a sea, this deadly languor, that rose and rose and drowned his consciousness bit by bit. Sometimes he was all but submerged, swimming through oblivion with a faltering stroke; and again, by some strange alchemy of soul, he would find another shred of will and strike out more strongly.

Without movement he lay on his back, and he could hear, slowly drawing near and nearer, the wheezing intake and output of the sick wolf's breath. It drew closer, ever closer, through an infinitude of time, and he did not move. It was at his ear. The harsh dry tongue grated like sandpaper against his cheek. His hands shot out—or at least he willed them to shoot out. The fingers were curved like talons, but they closed on empty air. Swiftness and certitude require strength, and the man had not this strength.

The patience of the wolf was terrible. The man's patience was no less terrible. For half a day he lay motionless, fighting off unconsciousness and waiting for the thing that was to feed upon him and upon which he wished to feed. Sometimes the languid sea rose over him and he dreamed long dreams; but ever through it all, waking and dreaming, he waited for the wheezing breath and the harsh caress of the tongue.

He did not hear the breath, and he slipped slowly from some dream to the feel of the tongue along his hand. He waited. The fangs pressed softly; the pressure increased; the wolf was exerting its last strength in an effort to sink teeth in the food for which it had waited so long. But the man had waited long, and the lacerated hand closed on the jaw. Slowly, while the wolf struggled feebly and the hand clutched feebly, the other hand crept across to a grip. Five minutes later the whole weight of the man's body was on top of the wolf. The hands had not sufficient strength to choke the wolf, but the face of the man was pressed close to the throat of the wolf and the mouth of the man was full of hair. At the end of half an hour the man was aware of a warm trickle in his throat. It was not pleasant. It was like molten lead being forced into his stomach, and it was forced by his will alone. Later the man rolled over on his back and slept.

There were some members of a scientific expedition on the whale-ship *Bedford*. From the deck they remarked a strange object on the shore. It was moving down the beach toward the water. They were unable to classify it, and, being scientific men, they climbed into the whale-boat alongside and went ashore to see. And they saw something that was alive but which could hardly be called a man. It was blind, unconscious. It squirmed along the ground like some monstrous worm. Most of its efforts were ineffectual, but it was persistent, and it writhed and twisted and went ahead perhaps a score of feet an hour.

Three weeks afterward the man lay in a bunk on the whale-ship *Bedford*, and with tears streaming down his wasted cheeks told who he was and what he had undergone. He also babbled incoherently of his mother, of sunny Southern California, and a home among the orange groves and flowers.

The days were not many after that when he sat at table with the scientific men and ship's officers. He gloated over the spectacle of so much food, watching it anxiously as it went into the mouths of others. With the disappearance of each mouthful an expression of deep regret came into his eyes. He was quite sane, yet he hated those men at mealtime. He was haunted by a fear that the food would not last. He inquired of the cook, the cabin-boy, the captain, concerning the food stores. They reassured him countless times; but he could not believe them, and pried cunningly about the lazarette to see with his own eyes.

It was noticed that the man was getting fat. He grew stouter with each day. The scientific men shook their heads and theorized. They limited the man at his meals, but still his girth increased and he swelled prodigiously under his shirt.

The sailors grinned. They knew. And when the scientific men set a watch on the man, they knew too. They saw him slouch for'ard after breakfast, and, like a mendicant, with outstretched palm, accost a sailor. The sailor grinned and passed him a fragment of sea biscuit. He clutched it avariciously, looked at it as a miser looks at gold, and thrust it into his shirt bosom. Similar were the donations from other grinning sailors.

The scientific men were discreet. They let him alone. But they privily examined his bunk. It was lined with hardtack; the mattress was stuffed with hardtack; every nook and cranny was filled with hardtack. Yet he was sane. He was taking precautions against another possible famine—that was all. He would recover from it, the scientific men said; and he did, ere the *Bedford's* anchor rumbled down in San Francisco Bay.

## THE WHITE MAN'S WAY

"TO cook by your fire and to sleep under your roof for the night," I had announced on entering old Ebbits's cabin; and he had looked at me blear-eyed and vacuous, while Zilla had favored me with a sour face and a contemptuous grunt. Zilla was his wife, and no more bitter-tongued, implacable old squaw dwelt on the Yukon. Nor would I have stopped there had my dogs been less tired or had the rest of the village been inhabited. But this cabin alone had I found occupied, and in this cabin, perforce, I took my shelter.

Old Ebbits now and again pulled his tangled wits together, and hints and sparkles of intelligence came and went in his eyes. Several times during the preparation of my supper he even essayed hospitable inquiries about my health, the condition and number of my dogs, and the distance I had travelled that day. And each time Zilla had looked sourer than ever and grunted more contemptuously.

Yet I confess that there was no particular call for cheerfulness on their part. There they crouched by the fire, the pair of them, at the end of their days, old and withered and helpless, racked by rheumatism, bitten by hunger, and tantalized by the frying-odors of my abundance of meat. They rocked back and forth in a slow and hopeless way, and regularly, once every five minutes, Ebbits emitted a low groan. It was not so much a groan of pain, as of pain-weariness. He was oppressed by the weight and the torment of this thing called life, and still more was he oppressed by the fear of death. His was that eternal tragedy of the aged, with whom the joy of life has departed and the instinct for death has not come.

When my moose-meat spluttered rowdily in the frying-pan, I noticed old Ebbits's nostrils twitch and distend as he caught the food-scent. He ceased rocking for a space and forgot to groan, while a look of intelligence seemed to come into his face.

Zilla, on the other hand, rocked more rapidly, and for the first time, in sharp little yelps, voiced her pain. It came to me that their behavior was like that of hungry dogs, and in the fitness of things I should not have been astonished had Zilla suddenly developed a tail and thumped it on the floor in right doggish fashion. Ebbits drooled a little and stopped his rocking very frequently to lean forward and thrust his tremulous nose nearer to the source of gustatory excitement.

When I passed them each a plate of the fried meat, they ate greedily, making loud mouth-noises—champings of worn teeth and sucking intakes of the breath, accompanied by a continuous spluttering and mumbling. After that, when I gave them each a mug of scalding tea, the noises ceased. Easement and content came into their faces. Zilla relaxed her sour mouth long enough to sigh her satisfaction. Neither rocked any more, and they seemed to have fallen into placid meditation. Then a dampness came into Ebbits's eyes, and I knew that the sorrow of self-pity was his. The search required to find their pipes told plainly that they had been without tobacco a long time, and the old man's eagerness for the narcotic rendered him helpless, so that I was compelled to light his pipe for him.

"Why are you all alone in the village?" I asked. "Is everybody dead? Has there been a great sickness? Are you alone left of the living?"

Old Ebbits shook his head, saying: "Nay, there has been no great sickness. The village has gone away to hunt meat. We be too old, our legs are not strong, nor can our backs carry the burdens of camp and trail. Wherefore we remain here and wonder when the young men will return with meat."

"What if the young men do return with meat?" Zilla demanded harshly.

"They may return with much meat," he quavered hopefully.

"Even so, with much meat," she continued, more harshly than before. "But of what worth to you and me? A few bones to gnaw in our toothless old age. But the back-fat, the kidneys, and the tongues—these shall go into other mouths than thine and mine, old man."

Ebbits nodded his head and wept silently.

"There be no one to hunt meat for us," she cried, turning fiercely upon me.

There was accusation in her manner, and I shrugged my shoulders in token that I was not guilty of the unknown crime imputed to me.

"Know, O White Man, that it is because of thy kind, because of all white men, that my man and I have no meat in our old age and sit without tobacco in the cold."

"Nay," Ebbits said gravely, with a stricter sense of justice. "Wrong has been done us, it be true; but the white men did not mean the wrong."

"Where be Moklan?" she demanded. "Where be thy strong son, Moklan, and the fish he was ever willing to bring that you might eat?"

The old man shook his head.

"And where be Bidarshik, thy strong son? Ever was he a mighty hunter, and ever did he bring thee the good back-fat and the sweet dried tongues of the moose and the caribou. I see no back-fat and no sweet dried tongues. Your stomach is full with emptiness through the days, and it is for a man of a very miserable and lying people to give you to eat."

"Nay," old Ebbits interposed in kindliness, "the white man's is not a lying people. The white man speaks true. Always does the white man speak true." He paused, casting about him for words wherewith to temper the severity of what he was about to say. "But the white man speaks true in different ways. To-day he speaks true one way, to-morrow he speaks true another way, and there is no understanding him nor his way."

"To-day speak true one way, to-morrow speak true another way, which is to lie," was Zilla's dictum.

"There is no understanding the white man," Ebbits went on doggedly.

The meat, and the tea, and the tobacco seemed to have brought him back to life, and he gripped tighter hold of the idea behind his age-bleared eyes. He straightened up somewhat. His voice lost its querulous and whimpering note, and became strong and positive. He turned upon me with dignity, and addressed me as equal addresses equal.

"The white man's eyes are not shut," he began. "The white man sees all things, and thinks greatly, and is very wise. But the white man of one day is not the white man of next day, and there is no understanding him. He does not do things always in the same way. And what way his next way is to be, one cannot know. Always does the Indian do the one thing in the one way. Always does the moose come down from the high mountains when the winter is here. Always does the salmon come in the spring when the ice has gone out of the river. Always does everything do all things in the same way, and the Indian knows and understands. But the white man does not do all things in the same way, and the Indian does not know nor understand.

"Tobacco be very good. It be food to the hungry man. It makes the strong man stronger, and the angry man to forget that he is angry. Also is tobacco of value. It is of very great value. The Indian gives one large salmon for one leaf of tobacco, and he chews the tobacco for a long time. It is the juice of the tobacco that is good. When it runs down his throat it makes him feel good inside. But the white man! When his mouth is full with the juice, what does he do? That juice, that juice of great value, he spits it out in the snow and it is lost. Does the white man like tobacco? I do not know. But if he likes tobacco, why does he spit out its value and lose it in the snow? It is a great foolishness and without understanding."

He ceased, puffed at the pipe, found that it was out, and passed it over to Zilla, who took the sneer at the white man off her lips in order to pucker them about the pipe-stem. Ebbits seemed sinking back into his senility with the tale untold, and I demanded:

"What of thy sons, Moklan and Bidarshik? And why is it that you and your old woman are without meat at the end of your years?"

He roused himself as from sleep, and straightened up with an effort.

"It is not good to steal," he said. "When the dog takes your meat you beat the dog with a club. Such is the law.

It is the law the man gave to the dog, and the dog must live to the law, else will it suffer the pain of the club. When man takes your meat, or your canoe, or your wife, you kill that man. That is the law, and it is a good law. It is not good to steal, wherefore it is the law that the man who steals must die. Whoso breaks the law must suffer hurt. It is a great hurt to die."

"But if you kill the man, why do you not kill the dog?" I asked.

Old Ebbits looked at me in childlike wonder, while Zilla sneered openly at the absurdity of my question.

"It is the way of the white man," Ebbits mumbled with an air of resignation.

"It is the foolishness of the white man," snapped Zilla.

"Then let old Ebbits teach the white man wisdom," I said softly.

"The dog is not killed, because it must pull the sled of the man. No man pulls another man's sled, wherefore the man is killed."

"Oh," I murmured.

"That is the law," old Ebbits went on. "Now listen, O White Man, and I will tell you of a great foolishness. There is an Indian. His name is Mobits. From white man he steals two pounds of flour. What does the white man do? Does he beat Mobits? No. Does he kill Mobits? No. What does he do to Mobits? I will tell you, O White Man. He has a house. He puts Mobits in that house. The roof is good. The walls are thick. He makes a fire that Mobits may be warm. He gives Mobits plenty grub to eat. It is good grub. Never in his all days does Mobits eat so good grub. There is bacon, and bread, and beans without end. Mobits have very good time.

"There is a big lock on door so that Mobits does not run away. This also is a great foolishness. Mobits will not run away. All the time is there plenty grub in that place, and warm blankets, and a big fire. Very foolish to run away. Mobits is not foolish. Three months Mobits stop in that place. He steal two pounds of flour. For that, white man take plenty good care of him. Mobits eat many pounds of flour, many pounds of sugar, of bacon, of beans without end. Also, Mobits drink much tea. After three months white man open door and tell Mobits he must go. Mobits does not want to go. He is like dog that is fed long time in one place. He want to stay in that place, and the white man must drive Mobits away. So Mobits come back to this village, and he is very fat. That is the white man's way, and there is no understanding it. It is a foolishness, a great foolishness."

"But thy sons?" I insisted. "Thy very strong sons and thine old-age hunger?"

"There was Moklan," Ebbits began.

"A strong man," interrupted the mother. "He could dip paddle all of a day and night and never stop for the need of rest. He was wise in the way of the salmon and in the way of the water. He was very wise."

"There was Moklan," Ebbits repeated, ignoring the interruption. "In the spring, he went down the Yukon with the young men to trade at Cambell Fort. There is a post there, filled with the goods of the white man, and a trader whose name is Jones. Likewise is there a white man's medicine man, what you call missionary. Also is there bad water at Cambell Fort, where the Yukon goes slim like a maiden, and the water is fast, and the currents rush this way and that and come together, and there are whirls and sucks, and always are the currents changing and the face of the water changing, so at any two times it is never the same. Moklan is my son, wherefore he is brave man—"

"Was not my father brave man?" Zilla demanded.

"Thy father was brave man," Ebbits acknowledged, with the air of one who will keep peace in the house at any cost. "Moklan is thy son and mine, wherefore he is brave. Mayhap, because of thy very brave father, Moklan is too brave. It is like when too much water is put in the pot it spills over. So too much bravery is put into Moklan, and the bravery spills over.

"The young men are much afraid of the bad water at Cambell Fort. But Moklan is not afraid. He laughs strong, Ho! ho! and he goes forth into the bad water. But where the currents come together the canoe is turned over. A whirl takes Moklan by the legs, and he goes around and around, and down and down, and is seen no more."

"Ai! ai!" wailed Zilla. "Crafty and wise was he, and my first-born!"

"I am the father of Moklan," Ebbits said, having patiently given the woman space for her noise. "I get into canoe and journey down to Cambell Fort to collect the debt!"

"Debt!" interrupted. "What debt?"

"The debt of Jones, who is chief trader," came the answer. "Such is the law of travel in a strange country."

I shook my head in token of my ignorance, and Ebbits looked compassion at me, while Zilla snorted her customary contempt.

"Look you, O White Man," he said. "In thy camp is a dog that bites. When the dog bites a man, you give that man a present because you are sorry and because it is thy dog. You make payment. Is it not so? Also, if you have in thy country bad hunting, or bad water, you must make payment. It is just. It is the law. Did not my father's brother go over into the Tanana Country and get killed by a bear? And did not the Tanana tribe pay my father many blankets and fine furs? It was just. It was bad hunting, and the Tanana people made payment for the bad hunting.

"So I, Ebbits, journeyed down to Cambell Fort to collect the debt. Jones, who is chief trader, looked at me, and he laughed. He made great laughter, and would not give payment. I went to the medicine-man, what you call missionary, and had large talk about the bad water and the payment that should be mine. And the missionary made talk about other things. He talk about where Moklan has gone, now he is dead. There be large fires in that place, and if missionary make true talk, I know that Moklan will be cold no more. Also the missionary talk about where I shall go when I am dead. And he say bad things. He say that I am blind. Which is a lie. He say that I am in great darkness. Which is a lie. And I say that the day come and the night come for everybody just the same, and that in my village it is no more dark than at Cambell Fort. Also, I say that darkness and light and where we go when we die be different things from the matter of payment of just debt for bad water. Then the missionary make large anger, and call me bad names of darkness, and tell me to go away. And so I come back from Cambell Fort, and no payment has been made, and Moklan is dead, and in my old age I am without fish and meat."

"Because of the white man," said Zilla.

"Because of the white man," Ebbits concurred. "And other things because of the white man. There was Bidarshik. One way did the white man deal with him; and yet another way for the same thing did the white man deal with Yamikan. And first must I tell you of Yamikan, who was a young man of this village and who chanced to kill a white man. It is not good to kill a man of another people. Always is there great trouble. It was not the fault of Yamikan that he killed the white man. Yamikan spoke always soft words and ran away from wrath as a dog from a stick. But this white man drank much whiskey, and in the night-time came to Yamikan's house and made much fight. Yamikan cannot run away, and the white man tries to kill him. Yamikan does not like to die, so he kills the white man.

"Then is all the village in great trouble. We are much afraid that we must make large payment to the white man's people, and we hide our blankets, and our furs, and all our wealth, so that it will seem that we are poor people and can make only small payment. After long time white men come. They are soldier white men, and they take Yamikan away with them. His mother make great noise and throw ashes in her hair, for she knows Yamikan is dead. And all the village knows that Yamikan is dead, and is glad that no payment is asked.

"That is in the spring when the ice has gone out of the river. One year go by, two years go by. It is spring-time again, and the ice has gone out of the river. And then Yamikan, who is dead, comes back to us, and he is not dead, but very fat, and we know that he has slept warm and had plenty grub to eat. He has much fine clothes and is all the same white man, and he has gathered large wisdom so that he is very quick head man in the village.

"And he has strange things to tell of the way of the white man, for he has seen much of the white man and done a great travel into the white man's country. First place, soldier white men take him down the river long way. All the way do they take him down the river to the end, where it runs into a lake which is larger than all the land and large as the sky. I do not know the Yukon is so big river, but Yamikan has seen with his own eyes. I do not think there is a lake larger than all the land and large as the sky, but Yamikan has seen. Also, he has told me that the waters of this lake be salt, which is a strange thing and beyond understanding.

"But the White Man knows all these marvels for himself, so I shall not weary him with the telling of them. Only will I tell him what happened to Yamikan. The white man give Yamikan much fine grub. All the time does Yamikan eat, and all the time is there plenty more grub. The white man lives under the sun, so said Yamikan, where there be much warmth, and animals have only hair and no fur, and the green things grow large and strong and become flour, and beans, and potatoes. And under the sun there is never famine. Always is there plenty grub. I do not know. Yamikan has said.

"And here is a strange thing that befell Yamikan. Never did the white man hurt him. Only did they give him warm bed at night and plenty fine grub. They take him across the salt lake which is big as the sky. He is on white man's fire-boat, what you call steamboat, only he is on boat maybe twenty times bigger than steamboat on Yukon. Also, it is made of iron, this boat, and yet does it not sink. This I do not understand, but Yamikan has said, 'I have journeyed far on the iron boat; behold! I am still alive.' It is a white man's soldier-boat with many soldier men upon it.

"After many sleeps of travel, a long, long time, Yamikan comes to a land where there is no snow. I cannot believe this. It is not in the nature of things that when winter comes there shall be no snow. But Yamikan has seen. Also have I asked the white men, and they have said yes, there is no snow in that country. But I cannot believe, and now I ask you if snow never come in that country. Also, I would hear the name of that country. I have heard the name before, but I would hear it again, if it be the same—thus will I know if I have heard lies or true talk."

Old Ebbits regarded me with a wistful face. He would have the truth at any cost, though it was his desire to retain his faith in the marvel he had never seen.

"Yes," I answered, "it is true talk that you have heard. There is no snow in that country, and its name is California."

"Cal-ee-forn-ee-yeh," he mumbled twice and thrice, listening intently to the sound of the syllables as they fell from his lips. He nodded his head in confirmation. "Yes, it is the same country of which Yamikan made talk."

I recognized the adventure of Yamikan as one likely to occur in the early days when Alaska first passed into the possession of the United States. Such a murder case, occurring before the instalment of territorial law and officials, might well have been taken down to the United States for trial before a Federal court.

"When Yamikan is in this country where there is no snow," old Ebbits continued, "he is taken to large house where many men make much talk. Long time men talk. Also many questions do they ask Yamikan. By and by they tell Yamikan he have no more trouble. Yamikan does not understand, for never has he had any trouble.

All the time have they given him warm place to sleep and plenty grub.

"But after that they give him much better grub, and they give him money, and they take him many places in white man's country, and he see many strange things which are beyond the understanding of Ebbits, who is an old man and has not journeyed far. After two years, Yamikan comes back to this village, and he is head man, and very wise until he dies.

"But before he dies, many times does he sit by my fire and make talk of the strange things he has seen. And Bidarshik, who is my son, sits by the fire and listens; and his eyes are very wide and large because of the things he hears. One night, after Yamikan has gone home, Bidarshik stands up, so, very tall, and he strikes his chest with his fist, and says, 'When I am a man, I shall journey in far places, even to the land where there is no snow, and see things for myself.'"

"Always did Bidarshik journey in far places," Zilla interrupted proudly.

"It be true," Ebbits assented gravely. "And always did he return to sit by the fire and hunger for yet other and unknown far places."

"And always did he remember the salt lake as big as the sky and the country under the sun where there is no snow," quoth Zilla.

"And always did he say, 'When I have the full strength of a man, I will go and see for myself if the talk of Yamikan be true talk,'" said Ebbits.

"But there was no way to go to the white man's country," said Zilla.

"Did he not go down to the salt lake that is big as the sky?" Ebbits demanded.

"And there was no way for him across the salt lake," said Zilla.

"Save in the white man's fire-boat which is of iron and is bigger than twenty steamboats on the Yukon," said Ebbits. He scowled at Zilla, whose withered lips were again writhing into speech, and compelled her to silence. "But the white man would not let him cross the salt lake in the fire-boat, and he returned to sit by the fire and hunger for the country under the sun where there is no snow."

"Yet on the salt lake had he seen the fire-boat of iron that did not sink," cried out Zilla the irrepressible.

"Ay," said Ebbits, "and he saw that Yamikan had made true talk of the things he had seen. But there was no way for Bidarshik to journey to the white man's land under the sun, and he grew sick and weary like an old man and moved not away from the fire. No longer did he go forth to kill meat—"

"And no longer did he eat the meat placed before him," Zilla broke in. "He would shake his head and say, 'Only do I care to eat the grub of the white man and grow fat after the manner of Yamikan.'"

"And he did not eat the meat," Ebbits went on. "And the sickness of Bidarshik grew into a great sickness until I thought he would die. It was not a sickness of the body, but of the head. It was a sickness of desire. I, Ebbits, who am his father, make a great think. I have no more sons and I do not want Bidarshik to die. It is a head-sickness, and there is but one way to make it well. Bidarshik must journey across the lake as large as the sky to the land where there is no snow, else will he die. I make a very great think, and then I see the way for Bidarshik to go.

"So, one night when he sits by the fire, very sick, his head hanging down, I say, 'my son, I have learned the way for you to go to the white man's land.' He looks at me, and his face is glad. 'Go,' I say, 'even as Yamikan went.' But Bidarshik is sick and does not understand. 'Go forth,' I say, 'and find a white man, and, even as Yamikan, do you kill that white man. Then will the soldier white men come and get you, and even as they took Yamikan will they take you across the salt lake to the white man's land. And then, even as Yamikan, will you return very fat, your eyes full of the things you have seen, your head filled with wisdom.'

"And Bidarshik stands up very quick, and his hand is reaching out for his gun. 'Where do you go?' I ask. 'To kill the white man,' he says. And I see that my words have been good in the ears of Bidarshik and that he will grow well again. Also do I know that my words have been wise.

"There is a white man come to this village. He does not seek after gold in the ground, nor after furs in the forest. All the time does he seek after bugs and flies. He does not eat the bugs and flies, then why does he seek after them? I do not know. Only do I know that he is a funny white man. Also does he seek after the eggs of birds. He does not eat the eggs. All that is inside he takes out, and only does he keep the shell. Eggshell is not good to eat. Nor does he eat the eggshells, but puts them away in soft boxes where they will not break. He catch many small birds. But he does not eat the birds. He takes only the skins and puts them away in boxes. Also does he like bones. Bones are not good to eat. And this strange white man likes best the bones of long time ago which he digs out of the ground.

"But he is not a fierce white man, and I know he will die very easy; so I say to Bidarshik, 'my son, there is the white man for you to kill.' And Bidarshik says that my words be wise. So he goes to a place he knows where are many bones in the ground. He digs up very many of these bones and brings them to the strange white man's camp. The white man is made very glad. His face shines like the sun, and he smiles with much gladness as he looks at the bones. He bends his head over, so, to look well at the bones, and then Bidarshik strikes him hard on the head, with axe, once, so, and the strange white man kicks and is dead.

"'Now,' I say to Bidarshik, 'will the white soldier men come and take you away to the land under the sun, where you will eat much and grow fat.' Bidarshik is happy. Already has his sickness gone from him, and he sits by the fire and waits for the coming of the white soldier men.

"How was I to know the way of the white man is never twice the same?" the old man demanded, whirling upon me fiercely. "How was I to know that what the white man does yesterday he will not do to-day, and that what he does to-day he will not do to-morrow?" Ebbits shook his head sadly. "There is no understanding the white man. Yesterday he takes Yamikan to the land under the sun and makes him fat with much grub. To-day he takes Bidarshik and—what does he do with Bidarshik? Let me tell you what he does with Bidarshik.

"I, Ebbits, his father, will tell you. He takes Bidarshik to Cambell Fort, and he ties a rope around his neck, so, and, when his feet are no more on the ground, he dies."

"Ai! ai!" wailed Zilla. "And never does he cross the lake large as the sky, nor see the land under the sun where there is no snow."

"Wherefore," old Ebbits said with grave dignity, "there be no one to hunt meat for me in my old age, and I sit hungry by my fire and tell my story to the White Man who has given me grub, and strong tea, and tobacco for my pipe."

"Because of the lying and very miserable white people," Zilla proclaimed shrilly.

"Nay," answered the old man with gentle positiveness. "Because of the way of the white man, which is without understanding and never twice the same."

# Jack London State Historic Park

Located in Glen Ellen, California in the "Valley of the Moon", the park includes the large ranch and buildings owned by Jack London that he purchased over a number of years in the early 1900's. It includes the museum, several buildings, and a number of ruins of old structures including the burnt-out Wolf House.

## Museum

The Museum was built by Charmian London after London's death in 1916. The House of Happy Walls was designed to be a museum as well as Charmian's home. She lived in the house from 1935 until 1945 (when she was not traveling abroad or staying with relatives). Today the museum includes displays in many rooms, with a complete set of first-edition books by Jack London, Charmian's 1901 Steinway piano, and many unique crafts and mementos Jack and Charmian collected in their travels.

This house is similar to the Wolf House in some ways—the Spanish-style roof tiles and walls of field stone, for example—but it is much smaller and more formal. Much of the furniture in the house was designed by the Londons and custom-built for use in Wolf House, though never used there due to the fire that destroyed Jack and Charmian's dream home. Several times a year small concerts are held upstairs in the historic building.

## Grave Site

During the last few years of his life, Jack London's health declined rapidly from the effects of failing kidneys. On November 22, 1916, at only forty years old, Jack London died after a brief coma. His death certificate states that the cause was "Uraemia following renal colic".

On November 26, 1916, in a silent ceremony, Charmian London placed her husband's ashes on the chosen knoll under a large rock from the Wolf House. After she passed away in 1955, Charmian's ashes were laid under the same rock, next to Jack.

## Wolf House

Started in 1911 and designed by architect Albert Farr, Jack's dream home was four levels comprising 15,000 square feet, 26 rooms and 9 fireplaces. It was constructed with beautiful locally-cut redwood logs, stone walls, and even contained a reflection pool.

Jack London wrote so many books about wolves and dogs that his friend George Sterling gave him the nickname 'The Wolf'. So when Jack started to build his dream house in 1911, it was only fitting that people would call it the 'Wolf House'.

Jack and Charmian never got to live in their home because one hot summer night in August 1913, spontaneous

combustion started a fire in the house. Nobody was living near the house so the fire was quite advanced before anyone became aware of it. The Londons were sleeping in the Cottage about a half mile away and were awakened by a farm worker who saw the red glow in the sky. They got on their horses and rode to their beloved dream house. By the time they got there, the house was completely engulfed in flames and beyond saving. Although Jack vowed to rebuild the house, he did not live long enough to rebuild. Today, we have a beautiful ruin.

## Cottage

The Cottage was London's principal home on the Beauty Ranch. This wood-framed cottage was purchased by London in 1911 along with the Kohler and Frohling winery buildings. It was enlarged after 1911 until it included some 3,000 square feet of living space. Here he wrote many of his later stories and novels.

In 2006, restoration of the cottage was completed and the re-furnished cottage and Stone Dining Room were opened to visitors. These two buildings capture Jack and Charmian's bohemian lifestyle and close working relationship.

## Beauty Ranch

The Beauty Ranch is the legacy of Jack's passion for the land. The Cottage, the Winery Ruin, the Silos, Barns and

Pig Palace are remnants of Jack and Charmian's life on the ranch. Combined with scenic beauty and miles of hiking and riding trails, the park attracts fans of the writer and nature lovers year round.

In 1905 London bought the first of several ranches on Sonoma Mountain in Glen Ellen, California. Using proceeds from his prolific writing career, London acquired adjoining parcels over several years and expanded his ranch, also known as the Ranch of Good Intentions.

By 1913 London owned 1400 acres on the slopes of the mountain and by 1916 employed nearly fifty workers building, farming, and tending prize livestock. Self-taught and inventive, London sought to improve farming methods using common sense, research, and concepts gleaned from travel. Visitors to the ranch today will see examples of his ingenuity and foreshadowing of organic and biodynamic methods popular today. He planted 65,000 eucalyptus trees hoping to use them for lumber but they eventually proved unsuitable.

The "Pig Palace"

## Lake

Jack London designed a stone dam on the slope of Sonoma Mountain, creating a lake at the headwaters of Kohler Creek. His plan, to capture water for his farming needs and to remediate erosion from the logged out hillsides above, worked well. He also saw the resulting lake as a cool respite for swimming and boating with Charmian and friends during the hot summers. The four-acre lake was completed in 1914 and became the topic of the first water rights trial in California. When London won the dispute, he invited all the neighbors for a barbecue beside the lake. The floating

walkway, along with piped in fresh spring water for showering, was state of the art in 1915. Charmian and other riders used the lake to swim their horses. During the Depression, Beauty Ranch was converted to a Guest Ranch that offered fishing, swimming, boating and picnics at the lake.

In 2010, London's lake was designated "one of the ten most threatened cultural landscapes in America". An assessment is underway to repair the dam, refresh the lake, and revitalize the adjacent wetland. These improvements will substantially reduce sediment downstream and provide fresh open water and wetland habitat for amphibians, reptiles, birds, and mammals on the mountain. Park visitors can still view the graceful stone dam and log bathhouse.

---

*I would rather be ashes than dust. I would rather that my spark should burn out in a brilliant blaze than it should be stifled by dry-rot. I would rather be a superb meteor, every atom of me in magnificent glow, than a sleepy and permanent planet. The proper function of man is to live, not to exist. I shall not waste my days in trying to prolong them. I shall use my time.*

—Jack London, 1916

# Map of the Park

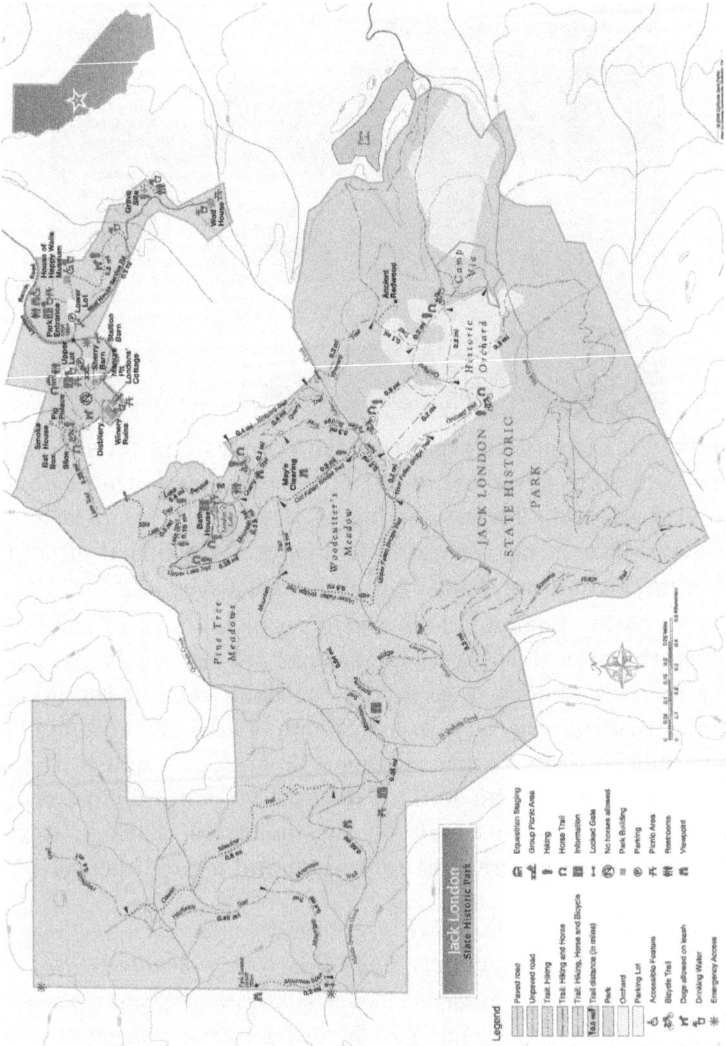

Made in the USA
Monee, IL
21 February 2023

28175669R00094